PROGRAMMED

A TRILBY BAINES NOVEL
T JENNINGS

LONE MESA PUBLISHING

www.lonemesapublishing.com

Contact the author at tjennings@tjennings.online.

THANK YOU

To M, my muse and my expert in all things…you.

To Linda, who read and commented on a work so… not you.

To Mandy, who read and commented with ghoulish glee.

To the few friends who may recognize themselves in these pages; everyone else should rest assured my friends' real lives are *not* this interesting.

CHAPTER ONE

WEEK ONE

Lieutenant Trilby Baines crept quietly around the exterior of a plain, one-story house, her pistol drawn. The front porch light offered a warm, welcoming glow that belied the terrified screams she could hear from somewhere inside. A child's constant wail; a man's staccato bursts, guttural and menacing; a woman pleading...

Trilby was first on scene, and as she waited on backup, she carefully circled the perimeter of the house, trying to get some glimpse into what was happening inside. Dispatch had received a 911 from inside the house—a woman screaming about her deranged husband, her children and a shotgun. The line disconnected suddenly. Neighbors called to report the screams. Trilby had been close.

"Dispatch, 512; show me 10-97." Trilby's radio squawked in her ear as Carlsen arrived on scene, immediately followed by Bailey and Moore. She was back to the front of the house and joined them near the squad cars.

"Whatcha got, Trilby?" Carlsen asked as he adjusted his bulletproof vest and double-checked his pistol.

"It sounds bad, Mike, but they're somewhere toward the interior; I couldn't see anything as I circled the house."

"SWAT?"

"I don't think there's time. From what I heard, we need to get in there fast."

"You're senior; your call."

Trilby pointed to Bailey and Moore. "You take the back. Be fast, but thorough. No shortcuts clearing the house just because we're going in hot."

She nodded at Carlsen. "You're with me."

They headed toward the front door, and Bailey and Moore disappeared into the darkness toward the back of the house. The screams inside were intensifying, and Trilby struggled against rising adrenaline.

As Carlsen braced to kick the door, Trilby turned the knob, which was unlocked. She took the time to smile at him before they swept inside.

Carefully, they checked the house room by room until they met Bailey and Moore outside the slightly ajar door to a dimly lit room.

"Shut up! Stop screaming! I can't hear myself think! I can't... I have to...Shut up!"

It was a man's voice, agitated and confused. Trilby could hear sirens in the distance and sent Moore back out to provide a report to arriving backup. She looked hard and Carlsen and Bailey as she listened to the rising pandemonium behind the door.

"We can't wait."

Carlsen nodded. They stood to the side of the door, and he tapped it open with the toe of his boot. Trilby prepared to swing into the room as the door opened when a shotgun blast blew through the opening door and tore a good-sized hole in the hallway wall.

"Who's there?! Who are you?! You leave! You leave now, or

I'll kill you, too!" Rage fueled every word.

She braced against the wall beside the doorjamb, breathing hard despite her best efforts. Stealthily, she lowered herself to the floor, kneeling to peek into the small office. The man held a small girl in front of him, crying and reaching for her mother. A woman kneeled at the man's feet, her face battered and a cut over her eye bleeding freely. She held another small child in her lap.

"Please!" she screamed suddenly. "Please, don't let him hurt her! Please save us!"

"Shut up, you! I already told you; no one is taking you from me—any of you!"

Trilby watched the man pace with the shotgun in one hand and the tow-headed child in the other. Sweat poured off his brow, as he jerked and twisted, scratching the side of his head now and then with the barrel of the shotgun.

He turned his eyes on the child in his arms. "Shut up! I told you I can't think!" Abruptly, he sat in a small wooden chair facing the door. He lowered his head and raised the gun to scratch his temple. The child took that moment to leap toward her mother.

He raised his head, and Trilby saw it—the wild rage of an animal, no humanity, nothing to lose. Before he could grab the girl or lower his gun toward any of the victims in the room, Trilby took her shot.

The bullet found him center mass, and he fell backward, taking the chair over with him. The woman grabbed both children and raced for the doorway, where Carlsen and Bailey gathered them up and lead them out to safety.

Trilby slowly entered the room, keeping her weapon trained on the suspect as she watched for any movement, but whatever madness had overtaken him was as dead as he was.

☐

As Trilby stood over the lifeless body of Jeffery Warren, the noise of screaming children and sirens gave way to the quieter bustle of the M.E.'s office and the crime scene techs. Her breathing returned to normal.

"You had no choice."

The voice came from behind her. Carlsen; she saw him in her peripheral vision and nodded. She had no doubts about the shot.

The scene played out in her mind in vivid color—the screaming toddler flinging herself free to reach her mother, Warren's shotgun leveling down to take aim, the space that left where he was unprotected… Trilby saw his eyes, wide, frantic, vacant, and then her finger squeezed the trigger. In an instant, the look in his eyes turned to shock and…relief?

CHAPTER TWO

Trilby looked at Chief Marcus McKay over the rim of her coffee cup as she took that much-anticipated first sip.

Sighing to herself, she enjoyed the hazelnut flavor—too much creamer, too much sugar, just the way she liked it—and she mused about how the caramel tone perfectly matched his warm eyes. Her sweet coffee was a personal joke between them, one of her "girlie" weaknesses.

As he read her file on the Warren case, she savored every sip, holding her cup under her nose to enjoy the aroma. While McKay concentrated on the file, he blindly reached for the coffee cup ever-present near his left hand. She scrunched her nose, knowing it was likely cold.

She knew the chief had already been behind his desk for at least two hours and had started his day by warming up yesterday's leftover pot. Had he needed a spoon, the midnight-black liquid would have dissolved it.

By the time she came into work at 8 a.m., the second pot of the day was brewing, and his generous use of coffee grounds made her cream and sugar all the more necessary. When she had a chance to fill the coffee maker, her go-to was a bag of gourmet hazelnut beans freshly ground, regardless of the flak she took from the other officers.

"What are you smiling at?" McKay cocked his head a little to the side as a trace of humor lifted his thick mustache at one corner.

"First cup of the day, Chief. Does a growing girl good." Trilby always took the first shot at her diminutive height. Confident and respected, she had nothing to prove.

McKay gave her one of his short-burst laughs, something between a single tone of amusement and an exaggerated sigh. He had almost a decade on Trilby, but he didn't look it. At 55, he remained strong and energetic, keeping up with the rookies rolling in out of the academy.

This was his second career in law enforcement. After taking his federal retirement five years ago, he joined the small Willow Creek police force as chief at the urging of the City Council.

Trilby came on board a year later, but she and the chief had been friends—and sometimes more—for almost two decades. They had lost touch during her tempestuous marriage but reconnected after her divorce and her career change—at 40 years old. Coming into law enforcement had been tough for a middle-aged, short-statured woman, but the fire inside her was a perfect match to the wild crimson color of her hair.

"You keep adding all that... stuff to your coffee, and you'll be growing right out of your uniform," McKay said, looking back at the open file on his desk. Trilby threw him a look anyway; he didn't have to see her to know her sentiment.

Trilby took another long, slow sip, ending with an almost purr. "Mmmmmmm."

McKay just shook his head and smiled. "You wanna tell me what's *not* in this report?" He looked up in time to see her feign innocence.

"There's no reason this file would be sitting in the middle of my desk this morning—after you pulled OT typing it up," he said, "unless there's more to the story because what I'm reading seems pretty cut and dried."

Another reason for Trilby's delight in the large cup of coffee was yesterday's 14-hour shift that ended when she dropped her report on the chief's desk. She had gotten little sleep before she had to climb out of bed this morning to do it all again.

"You tell me, Chief. Something doesn't feel right. We've had a week to run it down. File shows all the evidence I've got—everything I know and can prove…"

"But your gut's doing its little dance," McKay said.

Trilby's gut seldom led her astray on the job. Even as a rookie, she had been able to tell when a case still had threads that needed pulling.

McKay closed the file, took hold of his large coffee mug and leaned back in his oversized office chair. "So walk me through it."

Trilby rose to pace McKay's office as she thought back to the incident.

"Dispatch was for a domestic—drunk guy beating his wife and kids. Neighbors called it in. I was first on scene, with Carlsen, Bailey and Moore arriving 10 minutes behind me. By the time they arrived, I had done a perimeter check and was ready to go in. We knocked, got no answer, but could hear screaming from further in the house." She paused to take a breath.

"What about SWAT?"

"I couldn't see anything, but I could hear it, and I knew we didn't have time to wait on anyone else. It was my call, and I made it."

McKay nodded.

"Carlsen braced to kick in the door, but I tried the knob first, and it turned." She smiled at McKay. "I think he was disappointed."

"Sounds like Mike."

"Anyway, he went in first; I followed. We swept the house; found them in a small office toward the middle of the house."

Her speech was fast, her thinking faster, as she saw the incident play out in her mind's eye.

"We could hear crying and a man yelling. We stood off to the side, and Carlsen tapped the door with his foot. It swung open, and the deceased blew a very large hole in the wall across the hall from the doorway." She faced McKay.

"Turned out he had a shotgun. I ducked to the low part of the doorjamb and peeked around, saw that he was holding one of the toddlers in front of him, the woman was at his feet with another child in her lap, and she was in a bad way. By that time, the guy was screaming obscenities at us and threatening anyone who tried to take his family." Trilby shivered, her eyes unfocused as she relived the night.

"I watched him for a minute, noticed how he twitched, kept scratching his head with the barrel of the shotgun, sweat pouring off him. Typical junkie-look to him: unstable and unpredictable. That poor baby in his arms was wailing, and he was yelling at her to shut up. It was crazy loud, but when the woman called out to us, it all unraveled. Things were about to go nuclear."

She moved back to the chair in front of McKay's desk. "We had two choices—pull back and hope the guy calmed down and negotiators could defuse the situation, or take him out before anyone got hurt."

Trilby paused to search McKay's face. "I saw his eyes, Marcus, he had already gone over the edge, and no one was getting out of that room alive. When he raised the gun to scratch at his temple again, the little girl wrenched free trying to get to her mom. He started to bring the gun back down to take aim at her, but her movement opened a hole just big enough—"

"For a Hail Mary that could have ended very badly for you, the girl *and* mom," he finished for her.

She looked at him for a long, hard moment. "I never questioned that shot, and gut had nothing to do with it."

Trilby was a woman of faith. Both her department and the State Police had called it a righteous shoot, and the D.A.'s Office cleared her.

McKay accepted her answer with a nod. "And none of that is the reason this file was in the middle of my desk this morning."

Trilby sat on the edge of a chair in front of McKay's desk. She put her elbows on her knees, leaning toward her chief almost conspiratorially.

"Tox screen shows nothing in Jeffery Warren's system. Not drunk, not high. No history of mental illness and no medical condition that should have sent him into that kind of hysteria. By all accounts, he was a mild-mannered accountant—a boring, middle-aged man who doted on his wife and spent his weekends playing with his kids."

"M.E. has no theory on his behavior?"

"Not a clue." Trilby opened her hands in front of her in a sign of resignation. It was a puzzle that had kept her up all night, and she felt certain she was missing some key pieces.

"You know, Trilby, sometimes people just snap. The scenario is so common it's a running joke: 'He was a quiet man, kept to himself mostly. We never expected anything like this…'" McKay mimicked the common thread heard from any number of witnesses after violent incidents.

"I get it, Chief, but there's more here. I just know; this is not some guy who suddenly went off the rails…" Trilby sighed. "I gotta know, Marcus. There has to be a reason—any reason—why Jeffery Warren did what he did."

"You know as well as I do, Trilby, we don't always get to know the 'why.'"

"I know. I get it. But I'm telling you, Chief, we haven't heard the end of this one."

CHAPTER THREE

DAY ONE, EVENING

Trilby came through her front door peeling out of her uniform. Her heavy coat went into the hall closet, her boots beneath it. Walking into her bedroom, the gun came out. Her department-issue Sig Sauer was double-checked and locked away in a box at the top of her walk-in closet.

Her gun belt hung on a peg above a valet chair. She worked her way out of her uniform shirt and tossed it into the hamper, then hung her bulletproof vest on the chair. Everything else came off and went into the hamper as she made her way to the bathroom and a hot shower. There was something about washing away the day that helped her make the break between work and home.

Clean and refreshed, she dressed in a pair of running shorts and a tank top and headed for the kitchen. It had taken five long years to get used to the silence of living alone, and now she relished being in control of the noise and commotion she let into her home. She opened her fridge to a variety of plastic containers with lids, each holding the remains of some previous meal. In five years, she'd never learned how to cook for one.

She chose a light stir-fry of tangy vegetables and a bottle of crisp white wine and made her way to the microwave. With dinner warming, she poured herself a glass and felt the tension in her shoulders begin to melt.

She spilled her warmed-up dinner onto a plate and moved toward the couch. She turned on a lamp beside her seat and settled in to read; she was a sucker for romantic suspense. After a moment, she looked up and took in the dimly lit living room. Her style tended toward country antiques and Southwest décor. Nothing was out of place, although it needed a good dusting.

Trilby sighed. "Still miss the dog."

When she had to divorce her alcoholic husband, he left the Boxer behind, a sweet, clumsy brute. Trilby had agonized over giving her away, but with the long hours and no one to watch her, it had been better for Roxie. Trilby's house was cleaner and quieter, but that wasn't always a good thing.

She finished eating, put her plate in the sink and poured a touch more wine to take out onto the sunporch. From there, she had a beautiful view of the snow-capped peak, and she had buttoned up the porch for the winter so that, with the blanket she left out there for just such occasions, it was warm enough to sit on the wooden porch swing and contemplate life.

Just as she laid her head back and closed her eyes, she heard her phone. Her brow furrowed as she headed in to answer. "Baines."

"I know you're off duty, but I thought you might want to take a look at this scene while it's active."

She was surprised to hear McKay's voice, but then remembered he was filling in for one of his captains—something that sometimes happened with their small force.

"Why is that, Chief?"

"Domestic," McKay said. "Quiet guy, kept to himself mostly…"

Electricity ran up Trilby's spine. "Send a uni to pick me up. I've already had dinner."

McKay was familiar with her pattern of unwinding. "Be there in five."

"I'll put my dancing shoes back on."

☐

As she approached the room, Trilby studied the scene and the man in charge. McKay rubbed absently at his upper lip, just under his mustache, a habit he had whenever he was deep in thought. His eyes were focused, his expression guarded. Everyone had cleared the room except the two of them. He seemed far away, but she knew he had clocked her coming up in his peripheral.

At the center of the chaos in the room, a pool of blood congealed, surrounded by the refuse of an intense EMS call. Trilby knew from her experience with fire and rescue years before that the patient was either dead or working on getting that way fast.

"Whatcha got, Chief?"

Rather than her full duty gear, she wore a department polo with her BDUs and boots, no gun belt and no badge. She tucked her hair behind her ears, where the wind had left it mussed.

"Sorry to roust you off your comfy couch, but I was seeing too many similarities here."

"I was on the porch swing," Trilby said, smiling at him as she stepped gingerly into the room. "But you should be sorry; I had to put on a bra for this."

She was rewarded with his short-burst laugh again as he shook his head.

When Trilby first joined the force, she had a hard time with the banter at crime scenes, and like any outsider, wondered at the uncaring nature of her fellow officers. She soon learned the opposite was true; they cared too much. That moment or two of human connection—levity even—kept them on an even keel at the scenes of life's most horrific events.

They quickly set the banter aside and focused in on the scene. "Deceased is Kevin Jefferson, 45-year-old professor up on the hill—English Lit. Wife swears he's never been in trouble; loves her and the kids. Never any trouble in the marriage; the 'perfect' husband." McKay added air quotes around the word "perfect" because they all knew there was no such thing.

"Then tonight, he pulls a revolver out of the gun safe and threatens to shoot everyone. Wife and the cops on scene describe him as 'anxious,' 'agitated,' 'fidgety,' and 'paranoid.' I've got uniforms canvassing the neighbors."

Trilby looked up from where she squatted beside the blood pool on the floor. "Sounds familiar. Who called it in?"

"Neighbors heard screaming. When our guys arrived on scene and tried to talk to him, he barricaded himself in the living room, curtains drawn. Our negotiator tried to bring him out via cell phone, but the guy cut the connection and started firing rounds. Heat signature showed a clean shot, and the sniper took him out."

"Tommy's a great shot. I told you giving that 'squirrel hunter' decent gear was going to pay off someday."

McKay ignored the jab. "Luckily, Mr. Jefferson was a lousy shot. Wife took one in the arm—just grazed her. He missed the kids."

"Maybe. Maybe he was too crazy to aim, or maybe he just couldn't go through with it and fired the rounds to get himself taken out. And I take it from this mess that he was critical but not dead when you guys got in?"

McKay nodded. "Transported, but DOA. Suicide by cop? I suppose it's possible. Is that what you're thinking on Warren?"

Trilby moved to stand beside McKay, both with their arms crossed, surveying the room. "No idea what I'm thinking."

She patted him on the shoulder and turned toward the front door. "Hold down the fort, Chief. Thanks for the tip."

McKay smiled and nodded. "All done here, then?"

"I've seen enough. My PJs are calling my name…and the scene is in good hands. I'll borrow one of the guys for a ride home." She turned back to tip her invisible cap.

"See you in the morning, Baines." He smirked. "Try to behave yourself."

"Me? Always an angel."

McKay turned back to the scene, speaking just loud enough for Trilby to hear him, "She was a quiet girl, kept to herself mostly…"

He didn't turn around to see the look she gave him.

CHAPTER FOUR

DAY TWO

Trilby met McKay at the coffee pot the next morning and was delighted to find one of her coworkers had brought donuts. It would mean extra workout time, but it was worth it. Maple glazed was her undoing.

As she fixed her coffee and grabbed a donut, McKay stood to the side and watched. "You know we'll have to peel you off the ceiling in half an hour."

Her mania—sometimes fueled by sugar, sometimes the consequence of her crazy body chemistry—was a constant source of embarrassment for her and entertainment for the squad. McKay told her once that it must be exhausting to carry around all that explosive energy all the time. Usually, it manifested itself in fast speech, faster thoughts, and fidgeting, sometimes it was agonizing agitation, but she also got a lot of work done. She knew how tiring it was for those around her to keep up. Despite her condition, when the heat turned up, her focus zeroed in regardless.

"It's a chance I'm willing to take," she said around a bite of donut.

He shook his head, inviting her into his office with a grand sweep of his arm. "I've got the M.E. rushing results on Jefferson, but in the meantime, the canvas of the neighbors confirmed what the wife and family said: boring life, not a mean bone in his body. He was a soccer coach for his son's team and helped with the youth at his church; a well-loved citizen."

"No history of violence?"

"No history of anything. Clean as a whistle. He's never even had a traffic ticket."

"You're kidding."

McKay shook his head.

"Huh. Any obvious connection to Warren?" She settled into the chair in front of his desk.

"None that we found last night. We'll need to go back through the Warren side of things and see what comes up."

"Of course." She kept a notebook in her breast pocket and pulled it out to jot down a few thoughts. "Who's running point on Jefferson?"

When he didn't answer, she looked up. "Oh. Duh. Senior on scene. You know, you're kinda busy being the big-wig and all, you want me to take them both on—run them together?"

"I think I can make time to chase a few leads," McKay said with a smile.

Trilby put her notebook back in her pocket and considered her boss. Life had gotten considerably easier for her coworkers when she made lieutenant and earned the right to run all of the cases she was on. Trilby had a hard time letting someone else take lead, not because she bucked authority, but because had her own way of doing things. She was the first to admit that stubborn was a word she could have tattooed across her forehead; it would always apply.

She didn't intend to be difficult; she had an analytical way of looking at things that guided her through an investigation. The guys knew that whatever madness to her method, she tended to get results, so they stayed out of the way of her process. She and McKay hadn't tussled over any cases because they hadn't worked any together. She wondered how things would go.

☐

Trilby took to the Internet almost as well as her younger counterparts. However, after a few hours searching the farthest corners of even the dark web—and a few calls to her connections on both the state and federal levels—she still had nothing to connect the two men or anyone in their families.

She had also called some of the more helpful neighbors and friends from the Warren canvas to ask about Jefferson, but no one had ever heard of him.

McKay had gone to a luncheon with the mayor, and Trilby felt chatty, an urge to bounce her thoughts off someone just to hear herself think. Not wanting to subject any of the other officers in the squad room to her thinking aloud, she headed for the vending machines.

A few minutes later, she took the elevator to the basement, a *Dr Pepper* and a *Payday* candy bar in hand.

☐

Most cops avoided the morgue unless they had to be there. Trilby, with her background in emergency medicine, found it fascinating and had immediately made a lasting friendship with Medical Examiner Daniel Wilder. A large man of Asian descent, with a booming laugh and dark dancing eyes, Wilder delighted in every visit from Trilby—even when she didn't bring his favorite afternoon snack.

Willow Creek's wealthy tax base supported amenities most small departments couldn't boast—like a full-time medical examiner and a full-scale lab. As a result, they were able to avoid the backlog of cases waiting their turn at the state lab. To offset costs and keep Wilder busy, his department was also available to departments throughout the county.

As Trilby neared the morgue door, she could hear Wilder's nasally baritone carry through the room and into the hall. Unaccustomed to having any company, he long ago lost all concept of what her mother called an "inside voice." From the staccato cadence of his words, Trilby guessed he was in the midst of an autopsy.

As she walked through the door, she found him elbow deep in the chest cavity of Kevin Jefferson. "How goes it, Doc?"

Wilder jumped and almost dropped whatever organ he was handling at that moment. He turned, and his face broke into a large, friendly smile. "Ah, Trilby, what brings you to the dungeon?"

She raised her loot from the vending machine. "I come bearing gifts."

His smile widened. He set the organ in the basin beside him and began to remove his gory gloves and gown. "Delightful!"

They moved into his tiny office, and he shoved a pile of folders aside to make a space to set down his drink. "Not that I would ever look a gift horse in the mouth, but to what do I owe this immense pleasure?"

"I'm working the Warren case; McKay is on the Jefferson case. We think they may be connected. Have you found anything yet?"

"Unfortunately, nothing out of the ordinary, love." He took a long, slow drink of the soda and unwrapped the candy bar. "The organs all seem normal. Toxicology is still running. Nothing out of place on the external exam."

"I'm stumped, Daniel. I can't find a connection between the two, but the descriptions of the incidents…I'm betting dollars to donuts that tox screen comes back clean."

"I don't know what to tell you." Wilder took a dainty bite of the candy bar. "Nothing in their exams would have made me link them."

She rose to pace the tiny bit of office space not encumbered with equipment or furniture.

"I've got nothing linking them either—no friends, family, associates, associates of associates. No emails, texts, phone calls. They don't run in the same circles, belong to the same groups. Nothing about them clicks except that, by all accounts, they were squeaky-clean, average Joes, a couple of regular Mr. Rogers."

From around another dainty bite, Wilder asked, "Wasn't Mr. Rogers a Marine sniper?"

Trilby rolled her eyes. "Don't believe everything you read on the Internet, Daniel."

She paused. "But that's the point, really. Everything points to these two being the definition of nice guys, but my gut tells me there's more to the story."

She stopped pacing and looked Wilder in the eyes. "And whatever it is, Daniel, my gut says it isn't over."

☐

By the time Trilby reached the squad room, McKay was back at his desk. She barged in and took a seat.

"Make yourself at home." He closed the file in front of him to give her his attention.

"I was just down in the morgue. Daniel has nothing unusual on Jefferson."

"What about toxicology?"

"Not back yet, but I expect it to be clear."

"So, where does that leave us?"

"Nowhere." Trilby sat back with an exaggerated sigh.

"Still no connection between the two, other than you can't find a good reason for their behavior? I can't keep these investigations open forever…"

Trilby slouched down in her chair as much as her bulletproof vest would let her, laid her head on the back and put her hands over her eyes. "I know. I just need a little more time. There's *got* to be something here."

"Well, once the tox screen comes back, and I get Daniel's report…"

She looked up then. "I hear you, Chief."

▢

Trilby planned to run an extra mile as penance for her maple-glazed treat. She had just set her pace, earbuds piping Norah Jones directly into her blue mood, when the cell phone strapped to her arm began to buzz. She yanked it free and checked the ID—Carlsen.

"Baines."

"Hey, Trilby. Caught another domestic the chief thought you might want in on."

Trilby didn't like the sound of that and was ashamed by her immediate thought that it might buy her time on the Warren case. She tried to slow her breathing so she could carry on a conversation. "Where?"

It would take 15 minutes to the scene and another 10 to get out of her workout gear and into her uniform. She was probably 10 minutes down the trail. She gave Carlsen her ETA and headed back to the house at a fast pace. EMS was already gone, and the M.E. was done and removing the body, but the techs would be there for a while yet.

Trilby counted herself lucky to have a great trail meandering through the woods just behind her house. The path was level and smooth, even during snowy weather, so it provided a great place to walk or run. As she rounded the corner, she was surprised to see McKay's unmarked car in her driveway, the chief leaning nonchalantly against the driver's door.

She smiled to herself and kicked her pace up another notch. *He sure looks good in that uniform.*

Sometimes, Trilby wondered if she'd gotten over their two-year romance. It was hard to tell because their fondness for one another had transcended the physical element and remained, even during the years where they lost touch. But he had never lost the ability to make her heart skip a beat.

McKay saw her round the bend and removed his dark shades, revealing his soft brown eyes. She couldn't help noticing they traveled the length of her, taking in her tank top and shorts, despite the frigid weather.

He smiled. "Anybody tell you it's 48 degrees out here?"

She jogged past him and unlocked her front door, leaving it open for him to follow. "Not when you're putting out as much heat as I am."

"Amen to that," she heard him say under his breath as he turned away.

McKay followed her in and took a seat at the bar.

She faced him before heading down the hallway. "Give me 10 to sponge off and throw the uniform back on."

He rolled his eyes heavenward. "Get a move on, Baines. The scene won't wait forever."

☐

Carlsen met them at the door to a small suburban house, children's toys in the front yard. He led the two of them toward a back bedroom where they found an all-too-familiar bloodstain on the plush shag carpet.

"Deceased is Casey Miller. Medics did a load and go with a weak pulse, but they lost him before they made it to the ER."

"This is Chickasaw County jurisdiction, right?" McKay asked.

"Right, Chief. We came in as SWAT support."

McKay nodded for Carlsen to go on.

"The call came in as a domestic; neighbors heard screaming, which is unusual for this neighborhood. This back bedroom has no windows, and the deputies couldn't get Miller's attention inside. Having heard about our calls, they opted for SWAT. Since your fancy sniper couldn't get to him," he smiled at Trilby, "we went in prepared for the worst.

"We cleared the residence room by room, front to back and back to front and wound up here. Just like with Warren, he was pacing, talking to himself, and not paying attention to the wife or kids. In fact, it's like he's looking for someone—for us—to be coming through the door.

"I tried talking to him, but nothing he said made sense. He wanted the Sheriff. He said the Sheriff had to pay."

"The Sheriff?" Trilby gave Carlsen a quizzical look. "Well, that's different."

"Yeah. We were ready to try some kind of negotiation tactic when he looks down and sees the wife and kids trying to crawl toward a closet door. He turned the rifle toward her, and Cooper took the shot."

McKay nodded. "Make sure Cooper writes up his own statement on the shooting. So this guy was agitated like Warren?"

"Chief, it was like looking at his double—same pouring sweat and fidgeting, scratching like he was trying to get something out of his head. When the M.E. took the body, he said there were scratch marks at his temples where he had clawed at himself."

"And by all accounts so far, nice non-violent guy, right?" Trilby had her notebook out again as she asked the question, but she was looking at a bookshelf full of photos of the deceased and his family.

"You'd think the guy was a saint. Shoveled snow off all the walkways for the old folks in the neighborhood; ran the neighborhood watch; coached little league, you name it."

"Profession?"

"Stay-at-home dad. Wife runs a consulting business downtown for event marketing."

McKay looked at Trilby. "I guess your gut was right…"

CHAPTER FIVE

DAY THREE

Trilby spent the next morning following up on the Miller neighborhood canvas and contacting his close associates.

She was desperate to find a lead, but nothing panned out. She headed to the vending machine and then to the basement.

"Just as you suspected, dearest, not a smidgeon of anything hinky in his system."

Trilby sat on an empty examination table in the morgue as Daniel went over his results from Casey Miller's autopsy. She sipped her fifth coffee of the day, anxious and wired. "And nothing in his background or medical history to suggest a reason why he lost it?"

"Not a thing."

Trilby hopped down off the table and paced the morgue. "Daniel, what about their behavior? I mean, we saw what we all thought were classic signs of some kind of drug use based on the sweating and fidgeting at the scene and the severe paranoia."

She stopped in front of Wilder and stared up at the man. "Miller also *clawed* at his own melon, like he was trying to scratch his *brain*."

Daniel studied his report. "Trilby, I found *nothing* unusual about the brains of *any* of these men, and I don't know of any substance that could cause this type of behavior and not show up on toxicology."

"So you're saying there's *no* reason for three mild-mannered, middle-aged men to have suddenly become crazed killers, and yet..."

"I'm saying I see no known *medical* reason why this happened."

Trilby stopped her pacing and stared long and hard at the jovial M.E. before launching herself at the elevator. She heard him chuckle at her disappearing back. "Always in such a hurry, that one..."

☐

The guys in the squad room were used to seeing Trilby fly in as if her boots were on fire. They paid little attention as she raced to her desk and rummaged through stacks of notes, papers and phone message slips. Finally, she found the business card she sought and disappeared again.

She dialed the office number for Gwen Acosta, M.D., while the elevator headed for the first floor.

"I don't know why I don't have this saved in my phone," she grumbled, hitting send as soon as the doors opened. Trilby spoke with Gwen's receptionist as she headed to her patrol car and arranged to speak to the doctor following her current client.

She considered what to ask Gwen while she waited impatiently in the doctor's office. She paced the small space, looking at the myriad of photos and trinkets collected from around the world on Doctors without Borders excursions. Gwen's service to the impoverished around the globe was one reason Trilby found it easy to trust her, even if she was a shrink.

"Good afternoon, Trilby." Gwen swept into the room, tossing a notebook on her desk and settling onto a comfortable couch near bay windows on the other side of the room. She wore casual, but expensive slacks and a simple silk top, and tucked her legs beneath her before turning toward her guest.

It always surprised Trilby to see Gwen in her element. Accomplished and well respected, the psychiatrist looked younger than her thirty-something age, with a broad, bright-white smile most found infectious and disarming.

Trilby joined her on the couch. "Thanks for seeing me, Doc. I've got a weird one."

"I do weird all day. Shoot."

Trilby took a deep breath. "Is there a way for someone's thoughts to be completely altered from mild-mannered, nice guy to crazed murderer without the use of drugs?"

Gwen frowned. "You're going to have to give me more to go on."

Trilby nodded. She opened her notebook and began offering a sketch of behavior at each of the three scenes, including a basic overview of who each gunman was prior to the events. She didn't offer names or any information on victims, other than the involvement of wives and children.

Gwen thought for a long moment.

"Each of the men kept a firearm in the home?"

"Locked safely away…for protection."

"And you've found no connection between them other than the unusual behavior?"

"Correct. It's got me stumped, Doc. No one can give me a good reason why these guys lost it, and I've got a bad feeling about the future."

"All I can say, Trilby, is that programming that kind of sudden, violent personality shift would take time, expertise and…probably pain."

☐

David Fontane had another message from McKay. He was quickly running out of time to handle the situation. He knew he wasn't McKay's only contact with the feds, so if he didn't give the chief something on Kevin Jefferson, someone else would. He grabbed the phone and dialed with angry vigor. He'd just have to deal with whatever McKay managed to dig up…or with McKay.

"Hi, Dave, thanks for getting back to me. I hope you found something."

Fontane made his voice light. "Sorry, Marcus, it's been a madhouse around here. I've got some info for you, but I don't know how much help it will be. Jefferson was sent to a super hardcore discipline camp for boys. Privately owned. He spent almost two years there."

"Any idea why?"

Fontane knew why, but the records were sealed, even for an FBI agent, so they wouldn't have given him those details. Rather than give up the information on Kevin's violent childhood and how he ended his father's abuse—and his father—Fontane decided to stick to what he would have been able to ferret out.

"Particulars are sketchy; some kind of domestic violence situation."

"I see, Dave. Thanks. Do you have the camp name or a contact for the camp?"

Fontane ground his teeth but kept his frustration out of his voice. "The place was shut down more than a decade ago after some kind of scandal. Not sure there's anyone around anymore."

"Someone has to know something."

Fontane rubbed his forehead. "Maybe. I don't think there are more than 200 people in Parker, and who knows how many of them were around back then? Camp was named for the owner. Guy's name was Marvin Carlton."

"Parker? Really? That's not far from here. Wonder why I never heard about it."

"Like I said, place closed down before you got to Willow Creek. I guess there wasn't much talk about it after that."

"Ok. We'll check it out. Hey, Dave, I hate to ask, but can you run Jefferson's name against a couple others for me?"

Fontane's gut twisted. "Sure, whatcha got?"

"We've got a couple more cases we think may be related. Casey Miller and Jeffery Warren."

Fontane paused as if writing down names he could never forget. "Warren…Got it. I'll see what I can do. Listen, Marcus, this is starting to sound pretty serious. You guys need help over there?"

"I don't think so, Dave. At least not yet. You know I'd call you if we did. Thanks again. You're a life-saver."

Fontane hung up the phone, leaned his chin on his folded hands and stared at the closed connection. "I wouldn't bet on that, Marcus."

CHAPTER SIX

DAY THREE, EVENING

Gwen rescheduled her last meeting of the day so she and Trilby could talk an hour more. Then Trilby changed out of her uniform into jeans and a T-shirt she kept in her car for such occasions. They walked around the block to a little pub, both feeling the need to let loose and wipe away the darkness they had been discussing.

"Hey, Doc." Bev, a mountain of a woman in her sixties, gave Gwen a nod from behind the bar as the pair walked into her regular Friday-night watering hole. Gwen grabbed a booth near the pool table while Trilby stepped up to the bar to order a pair of chardonnays. One of a trio of bikers sitting beside her cocked an eyebrow at the dainty request, but her nod and wink disarmed any remark the leather-clad behemoth might have made.

On the way back, she stopped to lay a stack of quarters on the pool table to call next game and put a few more in the jukebox. She chose a selection of upbeat country and classic rock.

"Where everybody knows your name..." She sang softly as she handed Gwen her drink. Gwen slugged Trilby's arm playfully, then set her glass aside to grab the cue she had chosen. The previous game was wrapping up, and the pool table was open.

"Let's go. I believe you're up on me by two games."

Trilby took a long sip before turning to choose a cue. "You really need to learn how to let things go, Doc." She smiled big, chalking her cue and watching Gwen lean over the table to break.

The doctor had at least four inches on Trilby, tall and slim—built like a model with a model's face. Accustomed to turning heads, she paid no attention to the eyes that were on her now.

While Gwen ran the table, Trilby let her eyes float over the room, scanning it for threats and escape routes—always a cop. It was a light crowd, but a table on the other side of the bar held a group of about five college guys who looked to be throwing back a few too many.

Gwen came to stand next to her, and Trilby looked the table over; not a lot of stripes left. "I see you came to play tonight."

"As always, my friend," Gwen said, smiling over the rim of her glass.

They played three more games without incident, Gwen pulling into a tie with Trilby and then ahead of her with the third win.

"You're on fire tonight, Doc," Trilby sipped her only glass of chardonnay for the evening. The table across the room was reaching meltdown status, and her friend was in their crosshairs. "What say we call it a night, huh? Us working girls need our beauty sleep."

Gwen nodded and began to gather her things. Trilby turned to pay the waitress nearby, but behind her, she heard it.

"Oh, what's your hurry, beautiful? Let's you and me play a game."

She turned to see Gwen standing with her hand firmly in the middle of a young man's chest. She had a polite but not overly friendly smile in place.

"Oh, I think one of us has already been here much too long.

Why don't you let me call you and your friends a cab?"

Joe College reached out to grab her, putting his hands on either side of her waist. "Nah. How about you and me get out of here?"

He tried pulling her closer, but her locked elbow kept him at arm's length for the moment.

Trilby stepped closer. "I think she's right. Maybe we ought to get you boys home safe."

He turned an angry, confused face her direction. "Butt out. This is between me and my lady friend."

Gwen worked to pull free of his hands, but she was also backed up against the table with little room to maneuver. "My friend here is trying to help. You should really listen to her."

Now Joe College was mad at both of them. "Or what? What are the two of *you* going to do?"

Trilby had had enough. Out of the corner of her eye, she saw Bev pulling her bat from behind the bar and making her way around to the front of it.

"Junior, I'm trying to help here. Take your hands off my friend, go back to your group and pay out. I'll foot the bill for your cab and send you home. Last chance."

A drunken smirk turned back her way, followed by language that should never be applied to a lady.

Bev was almost within swinging distance, and his buddies had finally noticed what was about to go down across the bar from them. They were gearing up to jump in. Trilby kicked out with lightning speed, striking Joe College at the side of his kneecap and knocking him off his feet. He landed face down in the muck of the barroom floor, moaning. Before he could try to get up, she put her boot on the back of his neck and waved Bev toward his approaching comrades.

The woman turned, bat in both hands in front of her and a challenge written on her face that none of those boys wanted to meet.

"Hey! What the…Let him go!" they bellowed at Trilby from a safe distance. None dared cross Bev.

For his part, Joe College mumbled incoherently into the spilled beer and peanuts strewn across the floor.

"You boys have had your fun tonight." She grabbed her badge out of her back pocket, and when she flashed it for them, the flock of college kids froze. "Your friend here has been terribly impolite to us, and I think you should all make your apologies to Bev and her patrons and allow us to call you a cab since none of you thought to designate a driver."

A big guy at the front of the pack nodded sincerely. "Our bad," he said, jabbing an elbow into the boys on either side of him, who nodded quickly. "We didn't mean any harm." He turned to Bev and tipped his head. "Apologies, ma'am."

Her voice was raw from decades of cigarette smoke. "No harm, no foul."

Trilby released the boy under her boot, and his friends bent to help him up. Without looking up from the floor, he mumbled an apology, and the boys headed back to their table to settle their tab.

"I'll call them a cab," Bev said over her shoulder as she headed back to the bar.

"Thanks, Bev." Gwen straightened her blouse and gathered her purse from where it had fallen during the commotion.

"No worries, Doc. Part of the job."

Gwen linked her arm in Trilby's, and they walked toward the door. Near the bar, Trilby stopped and handed Bev money for the cab. The barkeep shook her head and smiled.

"You beat all, Baines. Soft-hearted cop."

Trilby put her finger to her grinning lips. "Don't tell anyone."

☐

As her headlights swept the driveway of her home, Trilby was again surprised; this time, McKay's personal car sat off to the side, and he was in the driver's seat with the engine running.

As she parked and headed toward the front door, he unfolded from the seat and fell into step behind her.

"To what do I owe this pleasure?" Trilby asked without looking at him.

"I thought I'd check in on you. Got a call from Acosta."

She looked back at him with a raised eyebrow. "And?"

"Sounds like quite a girls' night. Bev called to warn her that the kid with the bum knee was spouting off about police brutality."

She opened the front door and walked through the dark entryway without turning on any lights. A faint glow came from accent lights further on in her kitchen. The full moon poured silver light into her living room through a wall of windows across the front of the house and splashed it across them in the hall.

"He'll be fine, and he got off light. He was all over Gwen, so it was either me or Bev and her bat." She pulled off her coat to hang in the closet and set down the bag with her uniform in it, then turned to face him. "You came all the way over here to ask me about some punk kids at the pub?"

She had to look up into his dimly lit face. The emotion in his eyes was a mystery, half hidden by gossamer moonlight. They stood that way a long moment, and when he didn't answer, she shrugged and headed toward the living room.

"Come in and talk, then."

McKay let out the breath he hadn't realized he was holding. He had just come by to make sure she was OK. He wasn't even sure why, knowing full well she could take care of herself.

But he had followed her into the house and wasn't prepared to look down into her soft face in the moonlight. The glow caressed her pale skin, kissed her full, rose-hued lips and sparked soft highlights in her hair. Her bright blue eyes were more gray, deeper, intoxicating.

She was intoxicating, and he suddenly found himself lost in that moonlit vision, unable to speak, unable to breathe, doing everything in his power not to reach out and touch her.

When she walked away, he opened and closed the fists he had been clenching at his sides. *What is wrong with you?* He had no idea where that came from.

The lamp came on in the living room, and he looked to see her curled up on the couch watching him.

"Well?" If she had any notion of his current internal struggle, she hid it well.

He coughed and barely turned her way, but didn't move into the living room. "Nothing. Really. I just heard about the…issue. Was driving by. Looks like everything's fine, so I'm gonna go."

Now, her face showed confusion. "Yeah. Sure…Well, uh, thanks for checking."

"Sure, Trilby. Get some sleep. Try to stay out of trouble." He had meant it to be more of a joke, but even he heard the flatness of his voice.

"You got it, Chief." Her tone was unsure.

McKay forced his feet to move, his body to turn back toward the door. "I'll see you in the morning. You can fill me in on what the doc had to say then."

He didn't look back and felt as if he pulled against some unseen force just to cross the threshold and leave.

CHAPTER SEVEN

DAY FOUR

"Well, well now…This is an unexpected surprise."

McKay was shocked and a little unnerved to see Trilby at her desk when he arrived at work early—even for him. He had hoped to have time in his office to sort out his thoughts and feelings before he saw her again. He'd had no luck with that during the night and had given up on sleep by 4 a.m. A long jog followed by a long shower had done nothing to further his efforts.

He stood beside her desk sipping his coffee. "What gives?"

"Couldn't sleep. Case is getting to me, so I decided to come in and go back over my notes." Her desk was a mess of paperwork. He never understood how she could work that way, but she knew what every stack of papers held and had developed a system of abbreviations in her copious notes that was impossible for anyone else to decipher. She had a small filing cabinet beside her desk. He often wondered what she used it for.

She seemed tired but fine. Still, he had to wonder, *What's going through her head after last night?* He'd made a genuine fool of himself, and surely she knew it.

"Well, come tell me what you were after from Acosta." *Better to ignore the elephant in the room until one of us is ready to deal with it.*

Trilby grabbed her coffee cup and refilled it, then headed into his office. She settled into the chair across from his desk and took a long, slow sip.

McKay sank into his chair, leaning back, and looked his weary officer over. Maybe he was wrong; maybe she hadn't noticed.

"I got the final autopsy report on Miller. Daniel already released the bodies of Jefferson and Warren."

Trilby nodded.

"So, what sent you to the shrink?" McKay smiled. Acosta had served as the consultant psychiatrist for his department almost since he was hired, and he liked her. She got through to anyone he sent her way—meeting them on their turf.

"So, here's the thing. Something Daniel said yesterday when I was talking to him about the case made me curious. He said he had no *medical* reason for their behavior."

"And?"

"And what if there was a *psychological* reason?"

"You think something specific happened to make these guys snap, and you wanted Acosta to tell you what that might be?"

Trilby shrugged. "Makes as much sense as anything else."

"And?"

"She said *programming* them would take time, expertise and probably torture."

"Have you run across anything that suggests that might have happened to even one of them?"

"Not a thing."

"Trilby…"

She rose abruptly and headed for the door. "I know, Chief. I get it…"

"Wait." McKay paused for her to turn back toward him. "One thing did come up on Jefferson that has me curious."

She sipped her coffee trying not to look anxious. "And?"

"I told you there was nothing in his background…"

She nodded. "Yep. Not even a traffic ticket."

"Except that's not entirely true."

She sat back down.

"Nobody is that clean," He emphasized each word. "I made a couple more calls, and a buddy let me know yesterday afternoon—after you left—that Jefferson had some kind of expunged juvenile record lurking in his history. Not much to go on; some sort of domestic issue."

She leaned forward with her forearms on her knees. "Well, that's an interesting wrinkle. My contacts with the feds haven't found anything."

"My buddy only knows Jefferson did six months in some kind of boot camp to clear his name."

Trilby sat up so suddenly she just missed pouring coffee down the front of her uniform shirt. "Marcus, there was a photo on the shelf at Miller's house; I saw it while I was listening to Carlsen give his report. Not in a frame, just lying on the shelf with the other pictures. A group of about five boys, fifteen, maybe sixteen years old, wearing green camo BDUs and gray T-shirts. I figured it was ROTC or something, but what if—"

"What if that's the connection?" McKay was already dialing the phone. "I'll call Dave, see if he found anything on the other names."

☐

Trilby sat on Marjorie Miller's sofa with as much grace as her duty belt would allow. Holding a tiny china tea cup with two fingers, she sipped at the beverage she didn't want in an attempt to placate her host.

Marjorie looked frayed, not like a rope that's come untwisted, but more like the end of a rope slowly being burned away before Trilby's eyes.

"The kids are with my mother; we're staying there now… for a while…until we can decide…"

Trilby set the cup down and looked into Marjorie's eyes, waiting for her to finish.

"I was just here to get a few things, so when you called…"

"I appreciate you seeing me, Mrs. Miller. I am so sorry for everything that you're going through. I just needed to ask a few more questions."

"Of course." Marjorie seemed to shrink into herself at the prospect of talking about her husband's death.

"Mrs. Miller, when I was here before, I noticed a photo over on that shelf." Trilby pointed to an empty space where family photos had once been.

Marjorie turned to look. "My mother packed them away when she was here earlier. She thought it would help us…focus…on what we need to do in the house right now."

"I understand, Mrs. Miller. There was a photo loose on the shelf, not in a frame. Do you know what happened to that photo?"

"I don't know which photo you're talking about, Mrs. …?"

"Lieutenant Baines."

"Of course. I'm sorry. There was a photo not in a frame?" She rose and walked toward the hall closet, uncertainty in every faltering step. "I can't imagine…"

She took a box out of the closet and handed it to Trilby, who now stood behind her. "You're welcome to look."

Marjorie fidgeted with her hands, picking at the cuticles, which were already raw and scabbed. Trilby took the box. "Perhaps you might feel better if you got a little fresh air?"

Marjorie nodded, but her eyes were vacant. She shuffled toward the front door without even stopping to put on her coat.

Trilby took the box into the kitchen, but before she opened it, she placed a call to Gwen's office—now saved in her phone—and was assured the doctor was already out and nearby; she would drop everything and head Trilby's way. Gwen had a real gift for her work with victims, and Trilby felt Marjorie could use that help now.

That done, she opened the box and began to sift through the framed photographs of a loving, happy family. Somewhere toward the middle, she found what she was looking for. She found names written on the back—Kevin, Casey, Dave, Jeff, Donnie—and the words, "The Fatherless Five."

Trilby replaced the framed photos and pocketed the one of the boys. There would be no asking Marjorie Miller about the photo—not today.

As she headed for the front door, Trilby heard Gwen's faint voice, soothing and calm, leading Marjorie back into the warmth of the house. She had made good time getting there.

The two women walked through the front door, and Trilby saw that she had thrown her expensive fur coat over Marjorie's shoulders. She guided the distraught woman inside to sit on the sofa.

"We're just going to wait right here for your mother, and warm up." She kept her voice even and positive, but not light. "I'm going to sit with you until then."

She looked up at Trilby and nodded, her signal for the officer to make a quiet exit.

□

"Anything on the photo?" McKay had already set himself up in the "war room" when Trilby returned to the station.

"Widow wasn't in a good place to talk."

McKay nodded. "Can't blame her there. Maybe run it by the families for Jefferson and Warren? See if they recognize them?"

"It's a longshot, but I'll see what I can turn up."

Trilby settled in, and the pair spent the rest of the day and into the evening at the table in the large workspace set aside for major investigations. With magnetic whiteboards, its own coffee pot and water cooler, and a large conference table, it provided the perfect place to pour out the file contents on Warren, Jefferson, and Miller. Carlsen spent his shift on patrol but had given them everything he knew.

The photo of the boys joined photos of each man and crime scene photos on the white board. Time made it difficult, but it was still possible to recognize Casey, Jeff and Kevin in the fierce-looking teenagers. *So, where are Dave and Donnie?*

By late evening, the lines of the report Trilby was reading began to blur. The remains of their take-out food littered one end of the table, and coffee cups sat beside them, having been perpetually refilled over the last several hours.

Trilby put her head down on the table and groaned. "Nothing. No connections—not in the autopsies, the interviews, financials, cell phones, nothing."

McKay looked at her over the top of the file he was reading for the umpteenth time.

"You're done. Head home, Baines. It will all be here tomorrow."

She turned her head to the side, lying on her elbow, and gave him a dejected look. "Doesn't matter. I can't shut it off. Can't sleep. Whether I'm here or there, it's running through my head like some long-tailed cat I can't quite catch."

The simile made him grin. "Go home anyway. We'll head over to Parker first thing in the morning. Take the photo with us. It's a small town, lots of life-long citizens; something is bound to shake loose."

Trilby didn't move.

"Look, you're a wreck, and I'm tired of looking at you."

She stuck her tongue out at him. "I'm the best-looking cop you've got on my worst day, McKay."

Still, she sat up and tried to tame her unruly hair. It didn't take long for her to give up. Finally, she gathered up a few files she had been working on and carried them past her desk and out the door, thinking she wouldn't get much sleep.

☐

McKay watched her leave. He couldn't disagree with her argument. She wasn't the only woman in his department, but none of the others had quite the same effect on the uniform that she did. Unbidden, an image of her full, soft lips came to mind, and he shook his head to clear it. *Get it together, McKay.*

They had worked together for four years now as friends and colleagues, but sometimes, the memories of bygone days still got to him. Funny how he could remember those moments together so much easier than what it was that tore them apart.

CHAPTER EIGHT

DAY FIVE

McKay picked Trilby up in his unmarked unit the next morning. They dressed in plain clothes for the trip to Parker. Carlton Camp had operated on property about five miles south of town, so they hoped to find a few contacts who might know something about Carlton's activities.

The population sign said 203, and just beyond it, a faded, peeling billboard offered greetings from the Parker Methodist Church to any town visitors. McKay had driven all the way through what little town there was before he realized they were seeing the city limits sign.

He made a U-turn and pulled into a convenience store and bait shop next to the town's only stoplight. The old man behind the counter had to be in his 90s from the look of him. He sat on a three-legged stool watching the news on a 19-inch black-and-white television. Every so often, he spat into a coffee can on the counter beside him.

"Good morning," McKay said, as he approached the counter for directions.

The old man looked the pair up and down, spat, and then drawled, "Mornin'."

"We're from Willow Creek—"

"Well, I knew you weren't from these parts," the old man interrupted.

"No. We're from Willow Creek looking for some information on the Carlton Camp."

"That place has been closed-up nigh on twenty years now. Nothing going on out there."

"Yes. Yes, we know. But we're looking into a situation that may have ties to Carlton Camp—a man who may have been sent there when he was a teen, and—"

"Lord, it's a wonder he's alive at all then. What'd he do? Something terrible, I 'spect. That place…" He looked around as if someone might hear him in the otherwise empty store. "That place was chockful of evil, and the boys they sent there, they didn't come back the same… *if* they came back."

"Are you saying some of the boys died at the camp?" Trilby asked.

The old man drew himself up haughtily. "I ain't sayin' nothin'." He turned a suspicious eye on her. "Look. I don't know nothin'. You gotta talk to Elsa. She took care of Marvin and his…boy. If anybody knows what happened out there, Elsa knows."

After living through what seemed like an interminable period of hem-hawing and spitting and swearing their silence, the old man gave them directions to find Miss Elsa Cooke, former spinster housekeeper for the Carlton family and current resident of the Sunny Day Retirement Home out on County Road 9.

As they pulled up in front of the building, Trilby found the name completely misleading; the exterior of the facility suggested nothing sunny. Entering the building, the stench of disinfectant and despair seeping out of the walls confirmed her first impression. At the front desk, a middle-aged woman with a dour face offered them a permanent sour-taste pucker.

"Can I help you?" she asked, looking down her aquiline nose to take in Trilby from head to toe before looking McKay in the eye.

"We're here to see Miss Cooke, please." He gave her his most charming smile.

Her nametag read, "I. Hagge, R.N.," and Nurse Hagge was not impressed. "Miss Cooke never has visitors. Who are you and what do you want?"

Taken aback, McKay looked at Trilby and back. "Chief Marcus McKay, I'm from the Police Department out of Willow Creek; we're here on business."

Nurse Hagge looked back at Trilby with clear disapproval in her eyes. "What business could you have with a half-senile old woman in a nursing home?"

Trilby swallowed, unaware that she raised a hand to tame her always-tousled mane. The woman was more intimidating than Bev and her bat. "I'm afraid that's part of an ongoing investigation and not something we can share with you, ma'am."

"Humph. Well, you're going to have to talk to Elsa's doctor before you go traipsing back there and get her all worked up."

She reached over to the phone and dialed an inside line. "Dr. White, there are some…people here to see Elsa Cooke. They say they are with law enforcement." She eyed Trilby as she listened to the other end. "Of course, Doctor."

"Follow me," she said, rising to lead Trilby and McKay down a corridor to the doctor's office. She knocked but didn't wait before opening the door and leading them in. "Have a seat. He'll be right in."

McKay took a seat as the nurse left. Trilby walked the office looking at the photos and certificates on the walls. She reached to pick up a photo of the doctor with young boys, and the office door opened.

"Good afternoon. I'm sorry to keep you waiting. Nurse Hagge tells me you want to speak with Elsa Cooke?"

The doctor was much older than the man in the photo. She took a seat next to McKay across from the doctor's desk. "Yes. We were told she could give us information on Carlton Camp."

White's face fell. "Ah. I was afraid of that. I can't let you talk to Elsa… Not about…that."

"No?"

"That was a difficult time for her. So long ago. But it upsets her, and medically, I just can't let you do that. Miss Elsa will be 98 next week and still sharp as a tack but—despite what Nurse Hagge says—but in her case, that's no blessing. Her memories haunt her already. I won't have you stirring them up."

Trilby looked at McKay. *Now what?*

"What is it you wanted to know about the camp?"

Trilby turned back to the doctor with a questioning look. "We need to understand how the camp worked, what happened there and what happened to it…and what happened to the boys who went through there."

The darkness in White's eyes surprised her, then a lightbulb went off—the photo with the boys. "You were there? What, you worked with the camp?"

White sighed. "It's much more…complicated than that." He stared at his arthritic hands folded on his desktop. "Officer…?"

"Lieutenant Baines, sir. This is Chief McKay."

"Of course. Lieutenant Baines, I was sent to the camp at the age of 17. I stole a car, got caught, and my father—a well-known doctor—made a deal with the judge to have me carted off to Carlton Camp. I was locked away in that hellhole for 11 months, and that was in the beginning, before…"

He stopped and shook his head. He looked up, his eyes strained and pleading for them to hear the truth of what he was about to say. "Boys like me went through there for years. It was… It was Marvin Carlton's personal psychological experiment. He pushed us with pain and emotional torture—and he made us push each other. The things that were done to us—that we did to each other—no one should ever live through that."

Trilby slid Miller's photo to White. "Do you recognize any of these boys?"

He stared at the photo intently for a long moment. "There were so many… I don't know these boys, but that's the camp."

She took the photo back, nodding. "Who put a stop to it?"

White laughed. "I guess Marvin Carlton did." He looked up, his hands spread before him. "His son was one of the boys—one of us. The difference is we got to leave eventually; at least, some of us did. Some of the boys weren't strong enough, and…" His voice broke. "There's a cemetery at the back of the property."

Tears flowed down his face freely now. "But when I came in, Carlton threw his son in with us, and while we got to leave—one way or the other—Adam Carlton didn't. When I left, he was so broken."

White rose to walk to the wall where Trilby had seen the photo. "After I became a doctor, I volunteered to help at the camp—the boys who had a hard time, who might have ended up in the cemetery—they trusted me because I had been one of them."

He looked back at Trilby. "I helped Miss Elsa care for them as best we could, just as she had done for me.

"Over the years, I watched Adam take over, push Marvin aside, and twist what was already a terrifying experiment into something beyond damnation."

He walked back with the photo in his hand. "I knew I should have put a stop to everything, but you have to understand that… to survive…we did…things. No one came out of that camp wanting anyone to know about what we did." His tears fell on the faces of the boys.

"And then Adam Carlton killed his father." He looked up, and the terror in his eyes tore at Trilby's heart. "He killed him, skinned him, and hung him on the camp sign—right on the county road. When the police went in, they found the boys and the cemetery, but no one ever found Adam."

On the way back to town, McKay called Fontane but was forced to leave another message. "Hey, Dave. It's Marcus. I wanted you to know I got the info I needed in Parker today, even found a contact with a ledger of names on the boys brought into the camp. We'll be going over that tomorrow, but I'm sure we're going to find our guys on that list. Thanks again for the help."

Fontane listened to the message, his teeth grinding painfully, his vision a blur of rage. *Everything will be ruined.* He had to get that book; he had to plug the leak; and he had to get rid of Marcus McKay.

His brain fired on all cylinders trying to work out his next steps.

He knew there was no paper trail tying him to Carlton Camp, but there was no guarantee it would stay that way—not with people poking around in his long-dead business.

Fontane looked at the photo on his desk of his wife and kids: the perfect family postcard. Next to it was a photo of his parents. *The esteemed Senator George Fontane and his beloved wife, Emily, may they rest in peace.* His father's connections had made sure his son's…indiscretions as a youth had never found their way into the legal system, but George had also found a way to see to it that his son paid a hefty price.

Fontane lifted the photo off the desk to look more closely at his father's smiling eyes. *Did he know the price I really paid?*

His eyes closed against his will, and images flooded his consciousness. He could once again feel hot breath on his skin, his face pressed against the rough wood of the barn walls. "Do you really think he loves you, David? He sent you to me."

Fontane shook his head trying to clear it, but the fetid breath whispered in his ear again. "He *gave* you to me."

He clawed his way out of the memories. "How fortunate we are, *Father*, that McKay called me." He set the photo aside. None of it mattered now. All that mattered was making sure his secrets stayed secret.

☐

Trilby had a call of her own to make. "Gwen? I need a favor."

Gwen was fascinated by the case and more than willing to speak with Dr. White about his experiences at the camp. Trilby wanted to know what Adam did to program the boys—and how many there might be. Gwen wanted to know how they might help them.

"Gwen, don't let your big heart get you into trouble. You keep your eyes open and don't go wandering around Parker. Talk to White and then head home, hear me?"

Gwen was no shrinking violet, but she understood her friend's concern. She always carried pepper spray in her purse, knowing someday one of her clients might become a problem. She also trained in self-defense, and being an over-achiever, had attained a brown belt in Brazilian Ju-Jitsu despite her busy schedule. Still, she was tempted to add her Glock to that arsenal.

As soon as she'd broken off with Trilby, she had called to make arrangements with White. She would meet him in Parker the next evening—on his own turf—in an effort to make him feel more comfortable.

☐

After weeks with minimal sleep, Trilby all but fell into bed and was fast asleep in moments. Then, only a few hours later, she gasped awake in an ice-cold sweat.

She was frantic to remember what she had seen. The images were fading into fog more quickly than she could even out her breathing and rub the sleep from her eyes. *McKay?* She couldn't remember *seeing* him but felt he had been there, wherever *there* was, and he had been with something...dark. Trying to force a vision of the darkness made the hair on her arms stand up. *What was there? What did I see?* It was so infuriating to feel that she *knew* something, something sitting on the edge of her consciousness that her mind just couldn't quite capture.

Trilby put no stock in psychics and had never had any kind of premonitions or visionary dreams, but this felt real—like a warning.

There had to be a simple explanation, but she was at a loss as to what that would be.

Is Marcus in danger? Again the sensation of electricity up her spine. *No.* She had to figure this out. With no family left to speak of, no close friends since her move, there was no one—had never been anyone—who meant more to her than Marcus McKay. *No one is going to hurt him.*

CHAPTER NINE

"You look as tired as I feel." McKay met her at the coffee pot the next morning, surprised to see her so early again, already making the first pot of the day. Her uniform was in order, not a hair out of place, but there was a haunted look to her face accented by dark circles under her eyes.

She took the cup out of his hands and filled it with hot coffee. "It's fresh. I pitched that glop from last night."

McKay thought she meant some sarcasm, but her voice was flat, and when she raised her eyes to his, there was…concern? She looked fragile, and that scared him. He set his cup aside, took her hands and instinctively pulled her into an embrace. She laid her head on his shoulder with a sigh, her arms going around his waist.

"Trilby what's going on?" he said, his chin resting on top of her head.

"Bad night. Bad dreams. Bad feeling."

He pulled back enough to turn her face up and look into it. There was no one else in the squad room; none of the administrative personnel were on duty yet, dispatch was removed from this section, and the on-duty officers were out on patrol. It was eerily quiet, which is what he liked about coming in early.

The two of them stood that way a long moment, McKay looking

deeply into her tired, sad eyes. "How do I help?" he asked.

She pulled her chin free of his fingers and turned her face back into his shoulder. "Stay safe," she whispered.

McKay's brow creased. *Where is this coming from?* They stood together for a moment or two more, and then as if by silent consensus, they pulled apart and carried their coffee into his office, where Trilby told him about the elusive dream.

He smiled, trying to understand. "Trilby, we both know there's no reason to think I'm in any particular danger—beyond being a cop, that is. This is your body's reaction to too much stress, too little sleep and fried burritos right before bed."

His attempt at humor fell short. He leaned back in his chair and studied her. She was spooked. Whatever she had seen—but couldn't remember—it had hold of her, and he couldn't help wondering if it was going to affect her in the field.

"Look, Trilby, you know the job. We take every precaution we can to try to make it home at the end of the shift. Can't do more than that."

He tried to see the expression on her face, but her hair obscured it. After a moment, she sighed and looked up. "Enough of all that. Let's get to work. Did you get anything from your FBI guy on our other subjects?"

McKay remained silent a moment longer, reading the expression in her eyes, before nodding his agreement—back to work.

☐

Gwen cocked a brow at Trilby, who sighed. "I take it this is a working lunch then?"

"Spill it." Gwen had worked with Trilby for a few weeks after she was attacked on the job just a month in. The doctor wasn't one to stand on ceremony and procedure and had learned that, with Trilby, she was better off with upfront confrontation.

"I'm guessing the chief called you?"

"Yes, Marcus called. But even if he hadn't, I can see on your face that something is troubling you."

"It was just a dream…"

Gwen's face let Trilby know she wasn't getting out of this casual session over sub sandwiches and sweet tea.

"I don't really remember the dream. McKay was there…And he was with something…dark." Trilby shrugged. "Sorry, Doc. That's all I've got."

"But you feel like it means something?"

"I *feel* like it scared the pants off of me."

Gwen smiled at Trilby's quaint language. "And?"

"I just can't shake the feeling that Marcus is in trouble, but I'm no psychic kook."

Gwen waved the thought away with a dainty sweep of her hand. "Of course not. I know full well your opinion of those who claim to be so…gifted. But whether you like it or not, sometimes our subconscious pokes at us in subtle ways, like dreams. Science and psychology still struggle with the true purpose of the dream state, but I agree with the belief that at least part of the purpose is tackling problems—emotional, logical, whatever they may be—that your brain can't solve while you're awake.

"In my opinion, your agile mind is trying to tell you something. We both know you live half your life according to your gut instincts, and I think you should look at this dream the same way."

Gwen paused, tapping her lips, a habit she had when she was

thinking. "Yes. Yes, definitely. You know how I feel about intuition—conscious or subconscious—so follow your gut here."

Trilby shrugged. "I have no idea how I'm supposed to do that since I don't know what the dream meant."

Gwen sipped her sweet tea and smiled. "I'm sure your brain will let you know soon enough."

Trilby turned a sour look on the doctor. "Lovely.

☐

Albert Carl Holmes adjusted the small, oval glasses perched at the end of his nose, licked the tip of his finger and turned the page of a worn, well-read paperback. *Killer: A Journal of Murder* was by far his favorite of the many novels he collected detailing the gruesome lives of the world's most renowned serial killers.

"Mr. Holmes?" The bellhop stood at quiet attention beside him, waiting to be acknowledged. This unwavering respect for patrons was one of the many things Carl loved about the lavish hotels that he called home. He had grown bored with his last suite and sought a change. It was surprising the area had more than one upscale hotel, but he supposed it was an affluent community where global business was conducted daily.

Hamilton Howard Fish—The Gray Man—had preferred to be called "Albert" during his life of pedophilia, murder, and cannibalism. Carl, however, thought of himself by his middle name—lifted from the serial killer whose handwritten life story originated the book he held. Since none of Carl's names were real and people rarely spoke to him past business exchanges, it made no difference really.

"Is it unnatural that I should have absorbed these things and

have become what I am today, a treacherous, degenerate, brutal, human savage, devoid of all decent feeling..."

He was vaguely aware of the boy's discomfort; Carl Panzram's face stared angrily from the cover of Carl's book, and the image was certainly disturbing. He continued reading, *"...without conscience, morals, pity, sympathy, principle or any single good trait? Why am I what I am?"*

Carl knew. He understood the torture and pain Panzram had endured in a reform school that served as little more than a brutal juvenile prison. The experience created one of history's most horrific sociopaths. Likewise, Fish suffered beatings and punishment in an orphanage that programmed wildly deviant sexual desires in a boy whose entire family showed a history of mental illness.

Carl knew. He dragged his thoughts back to the boy in front of him and lazily looked up into the young man's expectant face.

"Yes?"

"Your room is ready, Mr. Holmes. May I take your bags?"

Carl smiled to himself. Holmes was the name of America's first purported serial killer. Carl often reread the accounts of Dr. Henry Howard Holmes and his "murder castle." Of course, even the infamous H.H. Holmes had been born under the unassuming name Herman Webster Mudgett.

What's in a name, really?

Carl placed a fine leather bookmark between the worn pages and closed his book. He put it in a hand-sewn leather attaché case before slowly rising to his full 6-foot height, only a little stooped with his advancing age. In his prime, he had been as big as Carl Panzram, although they did not share a love of tattoos. And where Panzram had been unapologetically evil—even to his cold, hard features—Carl Holmes tended more toward the description of Fish, a kind grandfather. The Gray Man had been small, but Carl's ability to mimic human compassion had diminished his frightening size to his early…playmates.

As he followed the slender, blond boy into the elevator, his inspection was discrete: the gray-blue eyes, the dimpled cheek—only the left—and the almost dainty slope of the nose. Not more than seventeen, Carl estimated, working his first real job judging by the lack of callouses on his soft hands.

When the boy looked his way, Carl smiled. There it was in the boy's eyes—trust. No one feared Carl…until it was too late.

Ah, thought Carl, *to be young again.* He had been younger than the bellboy when he took his first playmate—before he had been driven from his father's camp—his home—and the boys he loved.

☐

Trilby's description of Sunny Day Retirement Home was spot-on, and yet Gwen was taken aback by the overwhelming gloom of the place. It was after-hours—no nurse Hagge guarding the moat—so she rang the bell. A pleasant-looking, slightly older gentleman in a buttoned-down shirt and slacks let her in. His sad smile told her he was Dr. Stephen White.

As she entered, he offered his hand. "Dr. Acosta, I presume?"

"Dr. White, thank you so much for seeing me."

"Of course. Always good to spend time with a colleague; I'm a bit off the beaten path out here. I just wish it were under better circumstances."

"Of course." Gwen released his hand with a soft pat.

"Perhaps, we can speak in my office. It's a bit less…drab."

He indicated the way with a sweep of his arm, and Gwen followed.

"Do you not have a night staff?" The halls were dark, despite the early evening hour.

"We have a nurse and an orderly on staff, but they man stations down the other hall. This hall is all offices, storage rooms, and therapy rooms." He opened the door to his own office, and the soft light of dusk spilled out.

As she entered, she took in the simple, but comfortable surroundings. It was obvious White spent a good deal of his time there.

He indicated for her to sit on the plush sofa while he sat in a well-worn leather chair situated near a reading lamp and a table strewn with files and books. He noted her perusal of his office and smiled. "I try to keep it homey—both for the patients and for me. I don't have much else to keep me busy these days, so I spend most of my time here."

Gwen smiled. She wanted to earn White's trust before they got into the meat of the conversation.

"How long have you been with…Sunny Day, right?"

"Yes. Wretched name, isn't it? I wish we could provide an atmosphere more fitting, but as it is, the irony is not lost on me."

He leaned back into the plush leather and spread his hands before him. "I came here straight from residency, actually."

Gwen's surprise showed on her face.

White laughed. "I know. So many years in such a dismal place. Oh, at first, I traveled, medical missions and the like. We had more staff then—the town was bigger. But as the years passed and the money started to dry up, well, it's just me here now, and the nurses and orderlies. We're all that's left for the last few patients."

"The facility will close?"

"Yes, I expect so, as soon as Elsa is gone. None of the others bring in any funds, so if any are still alive, they'll be transported. Elsa's care is well compensated. Right now, it makes it possible to keep the doors open."

"Elsa?"

"Oh, I thought Detective Baines told you. Elsa Cooke. She was the...well, the cook, among other things, for Marvin Carlton. She cared for his family...and the other boys as she could."

There was a fondness in his voice that Gwen recognized. "And for you?"

He smiled. "Yes. Of course. And now, I care for her. I protect her—the way she tried to protect me."

Gwen heard the opening and took it. "Protect you?"

"Hmm," White said, his eyes going misty as if he were lost in his memories.

"I was there when Adam was first turned out of his father's house. I had only been there two months, and I was being roughed up every day by the other boys in the camp." White raised his eyes to Gwen, the pain in them tangible all these years later.

"Elsa took me into the kitchen to help, trying to keep me out of the yard as much as possible. And when things got too brutal, she nursed my wounds. I learned my love of medicine at that kitchen table." White managed a feeble smile. He rose and walked to the windows, the sun almost gone behind the horizon.

"Adam was just as lost and helpless as I was...at first. But he changed quickly, hardened, and soon took charge of the boys. In the hierarchy of camp life, Adam was our king, and for whatever reason, he took a liking to me. He kept me safe."

"Adam protected you? He didn't hurt you?"

"Well, yes, I suppose, sometimes. Adam could be quite cross." As White turned toward Gwen, his face took on the countenance of a lost child.

She nodded. "And the other boys?"

"Depends. Sometimes, Adam's methods were too extreme. I helped Elsa patched up the weak ones as best we could."

"What kind of methods?"

White's face went blank. "He said you'd come—that you would try to stop his plan."

The hair on the back of Gwen's neck stood on end.

"After my residency—which he paid for—he sent me here. He left me to take care of Elsa, but he told me you'd come."

"You're in contact with Adam?"

White smiled broadly. "I hadn't heard from him in years, but the money came like clockwork. And then, he called me today."

"Adam called you?" Gwen kept her voice even as she reached into her bag.

"Yes. He's been watching you and your…friends, and he is displeased." White walked toward the door. He closed and locked it.

Gwen closed her fingers on her cell phone, turning her body to keep White in front of her as he moved. She snuck a peek into her purse, swiped her phone unlocked and hit send on the last call she received. When she looked up, White was standing uncomfortably close.

"Is Adam here? Stephen, do you know where Adam is?" She hoped to buy some time using his first name.

White smiled again. "He didn't say, and I wouldn't tell you

anyway, but his plan is in play, and there are…problems. He said he needs my help."

"What kind of help does he need, Stephen?" Gwen was desperately looking for a way out of White's office. Despite his age, she could see he was in good condition. He was no more than two feet away, and she was about out of time to make a move.

"Well, he's sending someone for Elsa and me…and he'll be paying a visit to your lady cop friend, but he needs me to do something about you."

White's movements were still lazy, almost trancelike, but as he moved within reach of her leg, Gwen swept out and knocked him off his feet. She could hear Trilby's voice coming out of her purse, and she screamed. "White is with them! He's with Adam! Send help!"

She ran to the door, only to realize it locked with a key. She turned to find White back on his feet, the docile expression replaced with rage. "Adam said you weren't to be trusted. Such a little thing; how much trouble could you be?"

He leaped toward her, and she sidestepped him, bringing her elbow around to connect with his kidney as he barreled by her. She heard him grunt and go down to his knees. She turned to find him up on one knee facing her and kicked out hard, connecting with his shoulder and sending him back to the floor like a turtle on his back.

"You— I'll kill you!"

Gwen raised the pepper spray she had grabbed out of her purse and pressed the button. As White clawed at his flaming eyes, she dug into his pocket for the key.

She raced back to the door and had it unlocked and opened when she felt his hand grab her ankle and pull her from her feet. Still blinded, he subdued her with his full weight—at least 250 pounds at his height—and swung hard connecting with the left side of her face.

Her vision blurred, and pain shot through her head and neck. She pushed frantically at the brute as he grabbed handfuls of her hair and banged her head on the hardwood floor. Her ears rang, but she reached up with both hands and dug her thumbs into his watering eyes.

He screamed in fresh agony as he flung himself away from her. She scrabbled to her feet and raced toward the front doors and freedom. Just as she reached them, she heard the gunshot and felt the sting in her shoulder. It threw her against the glass, but she pushed the metal bar to open the door and used her momentum to race through. By the time she reached her car, she had her car key in hand and only barely registered the sound of sirens pulling into the parking lot.

She looked back toward the entrance to Sunny Day, where White stood, gun in hand. She clawed at her car door as he raised the pistol, frantically trying to work the lock. She heard another gunshot and subconsciously braced for the impact of the bullet. When it didn't come, she risked a glance back at White, seeing him crumple to the ground in slow motion, a strange peace spreading across his features as he fell.

She heard her name and tore her eyes away from White with difficulty. She saw Trilby lower her weapon.

"Gwen!" As Trilby ran to her, Gwen collapsed. Trilby caught her and lowered her slowly to the pavement.

"Trilby?" She felt herself struggling against sinking into shock; her pulse raced, darkness threatened the edges of her vision.

"It's ok, Gwen. I've got you."

"Is he…"

Trilby looked up to where Carlsen leaned over White's still body. He shook his head.

"He's dead, Gwen."

Gwen nodded. As Trilby waved the EMTs in their direction, Gwen grabbed her arm to get her attention.

"He was one of them, Trilby."

"One of who, Gwen?"

"Adam's boys."

CHAPTER TEN

DAY SIX, EVENING

Gwen looked tiny in her hospital bed. *This is my fault. I never should have involved her. I can't even imagine what she went through.* Trilby knew Gwen was stronger than she looked, but it pained her nonetheless. The shot to her shoulder was a soft-tissue through-and-through, so they took her into the OR for debridement and to be sure they had a handle on the extent of the damage. She had been out of surgery for an hour, and Trilby thanked God the injury wasn't more serious.

She had her head down in prayer, her hand holding Gwen's, when she felt the fingers move. Gwen was coming around.

Gwen coughed. "My throat is dry."

Trilby caught the eye of the nurse outside, who stepped in to check vitals. "She's thirsty."

"I'll get her a cup of ice chips, but be careful; she may be nauseated." She returned quickly, and Trilby took the cup from her.

Gwen allowed Trilby to spoon ice into her mouth.

"How are you feeling?"

"Like I got beat up and shot by a bear-sized psychotic doctor."

Trilby chuckled. "Well, at least your sense of sarcasm is intact."

"It's what you love about me." Gwen closed her eyes again. "Ok. Since the gunshot was a through-and-through, and the baby doctor has assured me that I'll live, I suppose I might as well answer your questions while I wait to get into a regular room."

Trilby smiled. "He isn't that young, Gwen." She quickly turned serious. "You were lucky. I'm so sorry I put you in that position."

"Eh. Scars are sexy, and I know a lovely plastic surgeon that does beautiful work, should I decide otherwise. I'll let them feed me horrible hospital food for a day or two, keep an eye on me to make sure nothing gets infected, and enjoy my wit and charm."

"You will be a *terrible* patient."

"Yes, I imagine so." Gwen opened her eyes. "OK. What do you want to know?"

"I don't need the full report now. You need to rest. Just hit the highlights, and I'll come back later to take a full statement."

"Sounds lovely."

☐

Trilby left the hospital with a little better understanding of Adam's "boys" and how he became the monster that still haunted them.

She called Carlsen first to get a report on any CSU findings from the scene at Sunny Day and White's house.

"Not much to say about his office that he didn't show you guys when you were there. We did try to speak to his Miss Elsa, but if she was lucid before, she's not now—probably at the doctor's doing. They brought in a team to check the patients, and whatever he gave her scrambled her brains permanently. We collected her records, and we're tracking down the account that paid for her care. Maybe that will take us somewhere.

"As for White's house, it doesn't look like he's even been there in weeks—fridge is full of unidentifiable substances that used to be food, rooms smell dusty and unused. There was a box of photos and papers at the top of his closet, and CSU took that back to the lab. We'll know more later."

Trilby's second call was to Daniel. "Ah, little one, how is your friend? I've always adored the lovely doctor."

"She's lucky, Daniel. Bullet hit nothing but soft tissue, through-and-through. They took her into the OR to clean things out, and she's resting now. They'll keep her a few days."

"That's good news then. I take it you are interested in my findings on Dr. White?"

"Anything you've got that can help me catch the monster that made him…"

"I wish I had more, Trilby. He suffered the same apparent abuse in childhood as we suspect of the others—broken bones that didn't heal quite right... No recent signs of injury—other than the cause of death and some trauma no doubt inflicted by the good Doctor Gwen."

"Thanks, Daniel. We know he was one of the boys tortured in that camp; he told Gwen that much. Your findings confirm that as well as our suspicions about the other men."

She was almost home when McKay picked up the phone. "Hi, Trilby, how's Gwen?"

"She's tough and lucky. She'll be ok. She insisted on giving me a report after she got out of surgery, but I kept it to the highlights. White was one of the boys who went through Carlton's boot camp, and he was there when Adam Carlton was first put into the dorms with the other boys.

"She said he suggested severe beatings and sexual abuse at the hands of other boys, and claimed Adam was his savior—who also terrified him."

"Daniel told me the autopsy suggested childhood abuse."

"Marcus, White told Gwen he hadn't heard from Adam in years, even though he's been paid to take care of Elsa. He hadn't heard from him, that is, until today…"

Trilby stood in the soft moonlight, the tank top and shorts she slept in exposing her to the chill of the night air. The wind rustled the treetops above her, and she caught the scent of honeysuckle in bloom along the white picket fence just visible in the farthest reaches of the pale light.

"Trilby…" She smiled as his arms slipped around her waist and the heat of his chest warmed her back. She felt him kiss the top of her head. "What are you doing out here in the cold?"

She leaned back into him and felt his lips caress the side of her neck. She smiled. "It's not that cold, and the moon is full."

He murmured against the curve of her neck. "It's warmer inside, and we can see the moon through the window."

She turned to look up into his face, and he kissed the tip of her nose as she wrapped her arms around his waist. "I can't smell the honeysuckle from inside."

He moved his lips down until they hovered just above hers. "You smell sweeter than the honeysuckle." His words, whispered against her mouth, made her heart race. "Come inside, Trilby."

A cloud moved across the moon, and darkness ate away at her vision. She felt him pulled from her embrace, and she reached for him desperately.

"Marcus, no. Stay."

"Come inside, Trilby…" The smile on his face hadn't changed, but he was…fading. The scent of honeysuckle was gone, replaced by the stench of charred remains, and as McKay moved farther from her, he became little more than a wisp of smoke.

"Come inside, Trilby…"

She woke screaming, clawing at the air as if she could take hold of the specter in her dream and pull him back to her. Slowly, she realized where she was—not the tiny home in New Mexico where she lived when she first knew McKay, when she first loved him.

The details of her bedroom slowly came into focus, and her breathing began to steady. Her bedside clock said 4 a.m., but there would be no more sleep for her.

Trilby sighed as she headed for the closet and pulled on a thick, full robe and slippers. Her eyes moved to the lockbox at the top of her closet, where her Sig Sauer rested. Something pulled at her to take it down, check it, and carry it with her into the kitchen.

"Running scared of bad dreams now," she said to herself as she laid the gun on the counter and made a cup of coffee. She sat on a barstool to drink the sweet hazelnut blend and stare at the gun. Finally, she lifted her eyes to her backyard, visible through the patio doors. "Something's gotta give, Lord."

☐

Fontane woke in an icy sweat. The fear on his wife's face told him he had lashed out in his dreams. Without a word, he made his way out of their bedroom and down the hall. Behind him, he heard the lock turn on the bedroom door. He stopped to look back. "Good for you, Patti."

In the guest bathroom, he stared at himself in the mirror—not the teenager he had been in his dream. He splashed water on his face and headed toward the guest bedroom. As he lay on top of the covers, not bothering to unmake the bed, he wondered why he didn't just set up shop in there; he had certainly spent more nights there than in bed with his wife. Patricia chalked his behavior up to PTSD because of the work he could never share with her. It had long ago inserted an insurmountable wedge between them. For years, they had maintained appearances for the sake of their kids, but what was the reason now? Their youngest left for college two months ago. Tomorrow he would rectify that situation.

He didn't think he had hurt her this time. Over the years, she had become a very light sleeper, and he suspected she had developed a kind of sixth sense about when the dreams would come. Less and less, she had fallen victim to his murderous dream-state rage.

Hesitantly, he closed his eyes, tried to even out his breathing and relax, but the images leaped at him from the darkness—crying boys, dirt and tears, blood. And Adam.

Adam was always the only clear point in the dreams. The boys melded together—too many to count, and had he ever really bothered to know who they were? But Adam…

"He *gave* you to me."

It had been hard and cruel at first, learning the truth about *George*—the truth about himself, who he really was. "He never loved you. I love you, David."

"But you hurt me…"

"And do you hate me for it? No. You want to be me, David. Just like me."

"No. No. I don't want to hurt them."

But he did. And he had.

"You cannot run from who you are, David. That's why he sent you here…Why he gave you to me."

"I'm not like you..."

"Of course not, love. You are you. I am the only one who wants you to be you, David. Isn't that what you want?"

"It isn't right…"

"Does it feel right?"

"It feels… Glorious."

Fontane's eyes flew open. His breathing was coming hard and fast, and he felt…alive.

Less and less, Adam had come to hurt him, and more and more, he had brought Fontane in to "play." He had taught him techniques, ways to hurt them without killing them, to take from them emotionally as well as physically. He had taught Fontane to relish in their pain, to feed on it until he needed it to survive—to breathe, to function.

"And then you left me." He spat the words out into the darkness like snake venom. Adam had become increasingly distant, leaving Fontane alone and forlorn for days on end. One day, George Fontane had arrived unannounced to collect his son. He packed up his son's few possessions and ripped him from the nest he had built at the camp.

As the car pulled through the front gates, David Fontane had turned to see Adam standing near the barn, a look of indifference on his face. It was only years later that Fontane had learned what happened at the camp and the reason his father had removed him before everything fell apart.

□

"Stop! Leave me alone!" Donnie Carter writhed within the tangled, sweat-soaked sheets, fighting to free himself from both the bedding and the man in his dreams.

He sat bolt upright in bed, eyes wide, breathing fast and heavy. His heart raced, and it took several moments for him to recognize the sanctuary of his own bedroom. He turned his head but knew Tracy wouldn't be in the bed beside him, and a tear traced the scar on his cheek as the full weight of reality set in. No wife; no kids down the hall; no life worth living anymore.

"I wish he had killed me then." Donnie's words rang with despair and hung in the darkness with the stench of sweat and fear. He bowed his head, but not to pray. Donnie knew no god; not one he could believe in anymore. Instead, he sobbed into the pitch-black, his heart rending again at all he had lost.

When his tears were finally spent and his body exhausted, he lay back into the tangled bedding, still afraid to close his eyes. The dreams had begun after Tracy died—after the cancer took her from him. That was only a few weeks ago, but it felt like a lifetime. Everyone had been able to see it—the darkness welling up in him, eating at him—and Tracy's folks had been right to take the kids. Donnie couldn't take care of himself, much less Katie and Carla. Their names in his mind twisted like a sharp knife in his gut.

Daddy, we don't want to go! We want to be with you! Carla didn't understand the evil growing in Donnie. He didn't want to lose his girls, but he couldn't risk hurting them, either. He wanted to die. He wanted to be with Tracy, and he wanted to be free of the man in his dreams—the face he had tried so hard to forget. Adam had barely been old enough to call a man. "But I was a *boy*! You and your...pet. How could I fight you? How could I—how could *we* stop you?"

Every night, Donnie sat in the darkness with his loaded pistol, unable to pull the trigger. Somehow, the evil he wanted to escape wouldn't let him take that path.

"Forgive me, Tracy. I abandoned our girls." His tears began to fall again, softly, and his eyes closed in weary, dreamless sleep.

CHAPTER ELEVEN

DAY SEVEN

Donnie opened his eyes with difficulty. His head pounded, and his stomach lurched. He reached for the whiskey bottle on the nightstand, but his arm refused to move. Confused, Donnie tried again, and the other arm, then his legs. He looked down to see his feet bound with duct tape and his confusion disappeared in a moment of abject horror.

Adam Carlton sat in a chair at the foot of his bed. Although it had been years since Donnie had seen him, Adam was the spitting image of his father. Donnie would have known him anywhere.

"Good morning, Donnie."

Donnie tried to scramble back from the apparition torturing his senses. *It can't be. It must be a dream. Wake up, Donnie!*

"Oh, do be still, you buffoon. I don't have time for all your silliness." Adam put his hand on Donnie's ankle, and Donnie froze, his eyes widening with terror.

"You... You aren't real."

"You will learn very soon, my friend, that I am terribly real. Have you missed me, Donnie?" Adam ran his hand up Donnie's leg to his knee and then grabbed his hands bound in front of him, pulling Donnie into a sitting position. "Because I've missed you..."

☐

"The most dangerous children are created..."

Trilby immersed herself in reading about violence and aggression in children. The subject sickened her. Since learning the men in her cases were connected as youths and had been beaten and possibly sexually abused, the idea of programming them for violence as adults felt even more right. They hadn't gotten anything useful on the methods from White, so they were back to figuring things out on their own. At least Gwen was safe and healing.

So far, Trilby had discovered that experts agreed— developmental neglect and traumatic stress during childhood resulted in violent, remorseless children more often than not. It wasn't hard for her to imagine the adults these children could become.

"One hundred billion neurons and one thousand billion glial cells...? What the heck is a glial cell?" Much of what she read was over her head. What she did get was that how a child was treated or what kinds of depravity he witnessed during his developmental years caused actual changes to his brain and its ability to regulate his behavior.

"So, if you intentionally harm a child, you could create a monster, but these guys weren't children... and they weren't monsters, at least not all the time."

Trilby often mumbled to herself when she was working her case files. The other officers had long ago learned to ignore her.

She turned her attention to another article suggesting 4-6 million children across the U.S. alone were at high risk for developing aggressive and antisocial behaviors, and that these early forms of aggressive behavior were the best predictor of later criminal behavior. "But it's still a leap from aggressive thug to programmed killer…"

Just finding the right keywords for an Internet search was stretching her creativity. She had to chuckle thinking about some black-ops government spy sifting through her search history. The intentional search results were bad enough, but some of the rest… "Good thing we've got a great anti-virus program."

Finding a solid link between programming via torture and triggered violence decades later was proving impossible, but she felt sure enough from what she did see to believe her theory was sound, and her gut told her the photo was a key.

She had a vague idea of how these killers were "created" and where, and it was a good bet Adam Carlton was in the middle of it since Carlton Sr. was dead. But why? It didn't make sense that Carlton came back after all these years to set these guys off just because he enjoyed it, and Trilby's gut told her all of it leaned toward an agenda they couldn't see.

After a long day of staring at her computer screen, Trilby's head was pounding. She slammed her fist into the middle of her desk, making her coffee cup rock dangerously. "What am I missing?!"

She felt a hand tousle her already messy hair. "Give it up, Baines. We'll get it, and we'll get Carlton, but you going blind at that computer isn't going to make it make sense any faster."

Trilby looked up into Carlsen's face. He offered her a bottle of over-the-counter headache medicine and a cup of water. "Those furrows across your brow tell me you've got a major headache going on. Take these. Shut down. Go home."

She just nodded and in a rare display of acquiescence, did exactly as she was told.

☐

"You live like a swine, Donnie," Carl said with utter disgust as he chose a filthy sock from piles of dirty clothes scattered around Donnie's bedroom. Empty liquor bottles and piles of cigarettes added to the disarray. He stuffed the sock in Donnie's mouth, then dragged him off the bed by his bound hands, pulling them over his head as they went. Carl heard one of Donnie's shoulder's snap out of place, but the sock muffled his scream as Carl muscled him across the room and into a large master bath.

"Tracy had such good taste, and it's a lovely size," Carl said as he switched on the light. At his wife's name, Donnie struggled against Carl's hold, attempting to kick his captor with his still bound feet.

"Tracy? Oh, but of course I knew her Donnie." Carl's tone was matter-of-fact as he hefted Donnie's girth into the oversized tub. "I sent her to you—to flip your switch, as it were, when your part of the plan came due.

"Oh, you wouldn't have even recognized her when I found her—just a whore in some back alley. But I saw her potential, and I taught her, groomed her into the wonderful woman she became.

"Such a shame, really, that she failed me."

Donnie gagged against the sock as he tried unsuccessfully to rail against Carl's accusations.

Carl sighed. "I suppose you have questions. All right then, I'll give you a moment to ask them, but do not test me, Donnie. You remember what happens when you test me."

He removed the sock and set it on the side of the tub. Donnie sputtered, trying to remove the fuzz and foul taste from his tongue. "What are you talking about, Adam? What plan?"

"Oh, the plan, well, I sent Tracy to keep an eye on you, make you love her and, keep you sane—you were always a little tightly wound. In the meantime, she made sure things were prepared for when I set things my plan in motion."

"Make me fall in love with her? Tracy loved me."

Carl smiled. "She was sociopath and an excellent actress, Donnie, but if it makes you feel better to remember your life that way, by all means…

"Where was I? Oh, yes, I got her the job with Denney, and she worked her magic to in close to him, make him rely on her. She was supposed to embezzle a rather large sum of money, and when Denney suspected her, she would turn to you to take care of him."

Carl smiled proudly. "We both know your volatile personality would have led to some serious complications for the esteemed banker. Alas, Tracy got sick, and everything was ruined. So much time wasted."

"You sick b—"

"Oh, if only! Had I been fatherless, we might all be different people, my friend."

"You made us like this, Adam, you and your cruelty. We were children!"

"Do you think I was *born* like this? Do you think the boys in the camp were my father's *first* victims? Don't be naïve, Donnie."

Carl's voice was full of venom, his eyes distant with dark memories. "I was *four years old* when my mother tried to take me away. We got as far as the woods before his dogs caught us, and he made me watch as they tore her apart. For years, I heard her screams in my sleep. She's buried in the garden, and she isn't alone—I had a brother who came and went before I was born…before my father learned how not to kill his toys."

Carl turned away to open a bag he had placed on the counter.

"And when he tired of me, he turned me out into the world of beasts he had created. But I knew—he had taught me—to survive, you must become a crueler version of the monster who made you."

He reached for the abandoned sock. "You really should save your strength, Donnie."

When he retrieved a propane torch and a fireplace poker from the bag at his feet, Donnie tried to scream and beg despite the gag.

"Yes. Yes. I know, Donnie. You want to tell me that you'll do as I say, whatever I say. You're already imaging the pain that's coming. But you know I don't believe you, Donnie."

Carl swept Donnie's sweaty hair out of his eyes and stroked his forehead tenderly. "No, Donnie. I have to know. I need to remind you so that I can trust you to play your part in the plan."

And Carl lit the torch.

☐

Carl savored a bite of his rare roast beef, washing it down with an excellent merlot. The dining room was dimly lit by an antique candelabra in the center of the large, mahogany table. He loved the old-world ambiance of his newest rooms.

"Ah, delightful," he said to no one. Carl was in the habit of talking to himself since he was rarely in the company of other people. "A perfect ending to a perfect day."

He relished the high as much as his gourmet meal. It had been so long since he had gotten to…play. He had meant to stay well clear of the boys (they would always be boys in his mind) once the plan was in motion—no ties to him—but he'd had no choice. He had to finish the plan, and he was running out of time. He had no idea how that pesky cop had figured out the camp connection, but he could feel her breathing down his neck.

He had gone to such lengths, too, putting Tracy in Donnie's path and then placing her at the bank, tutoring her meteoric rise. He was poised to "ruin" her just as she found out she was sick. Denney was sure to discover the embezzlement and fire her—despite their close ties.

Tracy would have ensured that her adoring husband—who undoubtedly would have believed anything she told him—was enraged and pointed straight at her boss.

Of course, Carl promised her escape, a tidy sum to start over with a new identity, leaving everyone and everything behind. His little chameleon; no one knew the real Tracy like Carl did. And it was all ruined.

"Fickle fate," Carl said into his merlot glass. He remembered the ragged, drug-addicted teen Tracy had been when he found her robbing one of her Johns at knifepoint in a dark alley. As he watched from the shadows, she cut the man's throat, her guttural diatribe against him and all of his kind a fitting backdrop to her heinous crime.

Since Carl had been in that same alley for other dark purposes, he felt the need to protect her from herself. He cleaned her up and mentored her in how to survive as a fierce predator in a world full of hunters.

"Such a pretty girl under all that grime, and a perfect student."

Something that might pass for sorrow crossed Carl's face. "Stolen from me before she could finish her task."

As quickly as the dark clouds formed, he swept them away with a flick of his wrist. "But all is well now. Not so elegant a solution, one must admit," he continued to himself as he cut another piece of meat, "but one must do what one must do."

He swallowed the bite with a sip of wine and smiled again. "And wasn't it fun to play with little Donnie again?"

□

McKay reached blindly for the offending noise on his bedside table. The clock read 2:43 a.m. "McKay."

"Marcus?"

He sat upright in bed, instantly awake. "Trilby, are you ok? What's wrong?"

There was a long pause, and then her voice came through, strained and meek. "I'm sorry. I feel so foolish. The dream was just so real…"

He rubbed a hand across his stubbled face. "It's ok. Take a breath and tell me…"

"No. I'm an idiot. Go back to sleep." The line went dead.

McKay didn't bother to lie back down. Instead, he set his phone aside and rose to pull on sweats and tennis shoes. He hoped this wasn't the break he worried about, but either way, he needed to get over there and talk to her. Trilby was no frail flower; if she phoned him in the middle of the night over a bad dream, he could only imagine what she had seen to make it feel that real.

□

It looked like every light in her house was on when he pulled into the driveway, but she had pulled shades across the windows in the living room—shades that hadn't been there a week ago, before the first dream. As he reached the front door, it opened.

"What are you doing here?" Her face was tear-stained and

weary, and she wouldn't look him in the eye. The Sig Sauer in her hand did not escape his attention, and he fought the desire to take it from her.

"I felt like taking a drive. You gonna let me in? It's kinda cold out here."

Trilby stepped aside, and McKay moved into the hall. She closed the door and headed toward the living room. She curled up on the couch, set the gun on the coffee table and took up the glass of chardonnay sitting there. In the dim light of the wood stove, her expression was hard to read.

McKay dropped his coat over the back of a chair and sat beside her. He laid his hand over hers, and they sat in silence a long while watching the flames dance across the stove's glass face. Finally, she leaned over to set her glass aside and then laid her head on his shoulder.

"Rough night?" he asked simply.

"I've had better."

"You always carry a loaded weapon around the house at 3 a.m.?"

"Only on rough nights."

He nodded. "I'll be sure to let you know when I'm coming by. You gonna tell me what has you so upset?"

He could feel her warm, silent tears begin to soak his shirt. He pulled his hand free from hers so he could wrap his arm around her shoulders. She snuggled against him, pulling her legs up onto the sofa and almost into his lap. She was wearing her tank top and shorts; he covered her bare skin with a blanket and waited for her to feel safe enough to speak.

"It was like the last two dreams…"

"Two?"

She had forgotten she never told him about the second nightmare.

"In the first, you were there with something evil; and in the second, it was like the evil stole you away—no, burned you away into a wisp of smoke. We were at the house in New Mexico, out in the back with the honeysuckle…"

McKay remembered those days well. He kissed the top of her head, almost reflexively. "And the pecan trees with the white picket fence…"

He felt her nod her head. "You told me to come inside, but then you… You just disappeared. Nothing but smoke."

"And tonight was worse?"

"Tonight, I followed you…the wisp of smoke…into a growing blackness, and then the blackness had teeth, and we were trapped inside this horrible, menacing smile…"

She rose up to look him in the eye for the first time. "There were others—only corpses, rotting behind the smile—and we weren't the last."

She looked so small, and her eyes were so large, only inches from his; the terror in them was real. McKay had no idea what to say. He didn't know how to help her, had no idea what was happening to her.

"Trilby, I…"

Tears formed in the corners of her eyes again. She whispered so softly, he barely heard her. "Marcus, I think I'm going crazy."

He pulled her into a tight embrace. "It's going to be ok, Trilby. I promise."

But he wasn't sure it was a promise he could keep.

Not long after she explained her dream, Trilby drifted off into a deep sleep. McKay carried her into her bedroom to lay her on the bed, but she clung to him in fear, so he lay down with her to calm her again.

He hadn't slept a moment since, feeling her body against his, her arm across his chest and her face nuzzled against his neck. It had been torture, but he kept his mind busy with any other thought as he tried not to disturb her.

Dawn was still somewhere in the distance when he felt her stir against him. Her hand slid up to touch his cheek, her face turned to kiss his neck. He wondered if she was still asleep.

"Thank you, Marcus…for staying."

"Um-hum," he said. He had to get out of there before something happened. His nerves were razor thin.

He felt her pull away and decided to make his move. He opened his eyes to see her raise up on her elbow. He was frozen. Her hair was ruffled and her eyes sleepy. She lifted her arm over her head in a lazy stretch, and his breath caught.

She heard it. Her arm came down, her hand back in the middle of his chest, and her eyes intent on his—a question he had to answer. He reached up and ran his hand along her jaw and into her soft, fiery hair, relishing the feel of it and the delicate scent released. Then he pulled her face toward his.

"Trilby…"

"I know." Her breath was as ragged as his.

His lips brushed against hers as he spoke. "This may be a very bad idea."

"I know."

He was in agony, every fiber of his being alive with a desire he hadn't let himself feel since she had come back into his life.

He skimmed a kiss against her lips, soft as rose petals, and felt his gut twist with indecision. "I really shouldn't…"

"Probably not," she said.

And then she kissed him.

McKay's body was on fire, his heart racing. His fingers twisted in Trilby's hair, his arm pulled her body close, and he hungrily returned her passionate kiss.

He felt her hand slip beneath his sweatshirt, and his mind exploded at her soft touch on his bare chest. He growled deep in his throat. He had never wanted anything—anyone—more. He deepened his kiss, and she moaned.

The sound electrified him, and he forced himself to push her away.

"Trilby…"

Her wild eyes looked back at him, her breathing hard and fast on his cheek. He had never seen a more beautiful woman. Every part of him wanted to take her, to possess her, but that part of him that loved her whispered, *Protect her.*

"I can't. Not like this."

She pulled away to look into his eyes.

He pushed himself up on his elbows. "We aren't who we were before; *you* aren't who you were."

He saw pain creeping in to replace the confusion on Trilby's face. He took her hand. "You're stronger, a woman of faith. Tomorrow, you'd regret this." His eyes pleaded with hers to understand.

She pulled her hand free and headed toward the bathroom to shower and dress. "It is tomorrow."

CHAPTER TWELVE

DAY EIGHT

McKay drove home to change for work. He couldn't get his mind off Trilby. He had left her in the shower without saying another word. What else could he say? *I don't want to hurt you again. I don't want to risk losing you completely.*

He knew he'd eventually have to say something; he couldn't let what had happened pull Trilby out of his life for good. And it wasn't fair to rip her life apart…again. He had to make her understand this was for her own good.

McKay was stepping out of the shower when the phone rang. Looking at the caller ID, he sighed. "Hey, Trilby."

Her voice was cold. "We've got a situation. SWAT is en route." She gave him the location and hung up.

McKay took time for one long moment of regret before he dressed and headed toward the call.

☐

Daniel's team was removing the bodies when McKay walked up. "Evening, Chief."

"Daniel. Whatcha got?"

"Looks to be a murder-suicide. ID on the deceased is Donald Carter; Carlsen said to call Trilby because he thought this guy looked like the 'Donnie' in your investigation photo."

McKay nodded. "The teen boys. Interesting that Carlsen recognized him."

"Not really. This guy was one of the older boys in the photo, and he hasn't changed much, I'd say." Daniel pulled the zipper on the body bag to show McKay what was left of Donald Carter's face. It was enough to recognize him.

McKay nodded. "So, another family hostage situation?"

"No. Not this time. Carter's victim is Victor Denney."

"The banker?"

"The very one. Shot at close range, once in the temple. Carter then turned the gun on himself. Wounds look to be consistent with the gun found at the scene. I'll know more after I get them back to the lab, of course."

McKay was already moving toward the front door. "Thanks, Daniel."

Trilby stood just inside, out of the way of the crime scene techs. Carlsen stood beside her. He nodded as McKay walked up. "Chief."

"Morning, Mike. Your call?"

"Lucky me."

McKay nodded. "Fill me in."

"I was just telling Baines, we got the call from Denney's neighbor. He heard shots at about 4:20 a.m. When we arrived, we got no response at the door. Team at the back could see the mess through the window."

Spread before them were two large blood pools on the carpet. Nothing else seemed out of place.

"Denney's body was bound with duct tape—hands and feet. From the position of the body, he appeared to be kneeling when

Carter shot him.

"Carter's body fell over Denney's from a position standing above the victim. A .38 Colt was found in a location consistent with having been held in his right hand for the shots. Two shots fired; two shell casings."

"Did he break in?" Trilby asked.

"Nope. Place is pristine except for right here, and the alarm was turned off," Carlsen said, nodding toward the blood. "Denney must have let him in."

"Did you run Carter's ID?"

"Yes. A couple of parking tickets and a report filed a month or so back—unit sent to his house on a noise complaint. No charges came out of it."

"So, this is one of the five…Where's his family? Why the change in behavior?"

"We sent units to his house. Neighbors said his wife died. Kids moved in with the in-laws. Said he fell apart after that."

An officer stuck his head in to let them know Denney's daughter had arrived. "I'll handle it," McKay said, turning to meet her outside.

The officer led him to a frazzled young woman with long, blonde hair and green eyes. She immediately latched on to McKay's arm. "What happened to my father?! They won't tell me anything! What's going on? The Burkes called me."

"The Burkes…are the neighbors?"

"Yes, yes. Tell me what's going on!"

"I'm sorry, Miss Denney—"

She corrected him, "Mrs. Malloy."

He nodded. "Mrs. Malloy. I'm sorry, but your father was

killed."

She crumbled against him sobbing, and he half-carried her to his car so she could sit in his back seat with the door open. He knelt beside the car to wait for her crying to subside enough for him to talk to her.

Handing her the package of tissues he kept for such emergencies, he asked, "Can I ask, Mrs. Malloy, if you know a man named Donald Carter?"

"Donnie? Of course. Tracy's husband. She worked for my father. Why?" Her look of confusion melted to one of complete anguish. "Donnie? Donnie did this?"

"It appears that way, Mrs. Malloy. Can you think of any reason why Mr. Carter may have wanted to harm your father?"

"No! The Carters were like family to us. We were devastated when Tracy died." She shook her head. "I knew… I knew Donnie was distraught after her death. We were all worried about him, and Tracy's parents took the children. But… Why…?"

"We don't know, Mrs. Malloy, but we're going to figure it out."

☐

Back at the station, McKay wanted to bathe in his coffee—take it intravenously if he could. With no sleep during the night and the tension of the morning, he was bone-weary, and the day hadn't even begun.

He left Trilby and Carlsen to follow-up on the canvas at both Denney's house and Carter's and dove into the pile of paperwork on his desk that kept the department running.

At about 9 a.m., his officers rolled in, grabbed their own jumbo cups of coffee and headed for his office. Feeling crowded in the small space by his guilty conscience and the pain behind Trilby's eyes, he moved the party to the war room.

Carter's photo joined those of Warren, Jefferson, and Miller on the whiteboard, as well as the photo of the five teens. Only one name remained—Dave. If only they had a last name.

After Carlsen put up Carter's photo, they all sat in silence looking at the faces of the men.

Carlsen looked from Carter's photo to that of the teen boys. "I'd say this is our 'Donnie.'"

Trilby nodded. "Him, I recognized."

"Well, this one is a big deviation from the other two." Carlsen replaced the photo and took his seat. "Carter's neighbors said he went off the rails when his wife died. Crawled into a bottle, became loud and belligerent. That's what led to the noise complaint—he was standing in his backyard screaming. When the unit got there, he was compliant, and his neighbor offered to put him to bed, so the officer left it alone.

"Not long after that, Carter asked his wife's parents to take the kids. When I notified the in-laws of his death, they said they weren't surprised. Said he was extremely depressed and suicidal from the moment his wife died. He decided he couldn't care for the girls and was afraid he would hurt them. Tracy's father said Carter told him he had nightmares about it."

McKay's eyebrows went up. "Well, that would fit with what we know of the others—at least the urge to hurt family."

He rose to pace the room. "So, if we're following your theory on programming, the wife's death threw a monkey wrench into whatever it is that triggers these guys…made him send his kids away, but then that shifted his target? Why?"

"Everyone I talked to backed up the daughter's story, Chief." Carlsen shrugged. "Said the Carters were like family to Denney. He was a widower with just the one girl. She has one kid—a girl. Neighbors said the Carters were at Denney's house more often than the daughter."

He pulled his notebook from his shirt pocket. "I put in a call to Denney's office. He was bank president. Tracy Carter worked for him for five years, winding up as manager in his trust department. Model employee; dearly loved. When she got sick, Denney helped with medical expenses, but it was stage-four breast cancer. Within a month of finding out, she was gone."

"Obviously, there's a piece missing someplace," Trilby said. She stood staring at the photos. "Something makes Carter different."

"You know, it would help if we had one clue as to why these guys suddenly wanted to kill their families," Carlsen said.

"I mean, maybe your programming theory makes sense, Trilby, I don't know, but the question is still *why*. What's the point of programming those guys to kill their wives and kids?"

Trilby turned to him, her face bright with a connection. "But they didn't kill their wives and kids… And even if they had, to a guy like Adam Carlton, those fatalities wouldn't have mattered one bit.

"No, maybe… Maybe the point of having them go ballistic in their own homes wasn't to kill their families, but to get themselves killed…"

"And their families would have been collateral damage in a suicide by cop?"

"Something like that."

McKay moved to stand next to her. "Why?"

"To protect the other boys… Maybe Adam thought it would

keep us busy and distract us, but it also conveniently dispatches two of the boys in the photo that would have known something about what happened."

"Two?"

"I think Miller had a target like Carter did. His situation looks like Warren and Jefferson, except he asked for the Sheriff. I don't know why, but I think that fits in. I think there's a plan in play that involves Miller, Carter and the other boy in that photo. My gut says there's something coming, something big."

The two stood shoulder to shoulder staring at the photos on the board.

"If you're right, there's one more lost boy out there waiting to be turned into a weapon."

"At least," Trilby said, nodding absently.

"So, where does the good doctor fit into all of this?" Carlsen asked.

"He's an anomaly—not part of the plan." Trilby turned to Carlsen. "Adam was using White to clean up a mess. We spooked him when we started snooping around. Maybe Gwen was a warning, or maybe she was the beginning of a new plan that we're not going to like much."

CHAPTER THIRTEEN

"Well, my. Curiouser and curiouser." Daniel stooped over the body of Donald Carter, intent on his work as Trilby sailed into the morgue.

"Do tell, Alice." Trilby's recognition of his literary quote earned her a broad smile from her favorite medical examiner.

"Ah, good afternoon, dearest. I presume you are here about Mr. Carter."

"And just in time, from the sound of it," Trilby pulled on gloves and a gown to step closer to the autopsy table for a better look. "Whatcha got?"

"Wounds consistent with possible torture." Daniel pointed to burn marks on Carter's stomach and thighs.

"Those are fresh," Trilby said with surprise. After discovering the connection to Carlton Camp, she had wondered about any missed scarring on the bodies that could have come from torture as teens but hadn't expected anything new.

"Yes, quite. Within days." Daniel leaned on the table looking across the body at his guest. "There's a chance they could be self-inflicted, I suppose, if the man had some superhuman pain tolerance, but I highly doubt it. My opinion would be that someone spent hours with Mr. Carter inflicting these wounds."

"Any other anomalies in his autopsy?"

"He was drunk as a skunk when he died."

"That may not be too surprising, given his recent history. What about any evidence of old wounds?"

"Not much that I could point to as suspicious, really. A broken arm, a broken finger… But I'm sure this is something." He showed her the inside of Carter's upper left arm. Carved deep into the soft, white flesh, were the initials A.C.

☐

"Trilby, can you come to my office, please?" She had barely spoken a word to him in days that wasn't related to the case, and it was driving McKay nuts.

"Of course, Chief," Trilby replied quietly.

He closed the door behind them, and she took a seat in front of his desk. He leaned against the front of it. "We need to talk."

"Nothing to talk about." Trilby stared into her half-empty coffee cup.

"Trilby, we have to get past this; we've been friends too long to just…"

She looked up then, waiting for him to qualify whatever it was they were doing—or almost did—but he had no idea what he meant to say. And the pain in her eyes cut him like a knife. It was the exact opposite of what he wanted.

He sat in the chair next to her. "Trilby, I don't want to hurt you."

She again looked down into her coffee cup, a sad smile on her face. "Marcus, I think you missed that mark."

"I—"

She held up her hand. "You don't want to get involved with

99

me…again…because you're still who you were—that guy who's never going to settle down with a nice girl—and I'm not the girl who will share you with anyone else…anymore. I get it. And you're right; I would have regretted letting things get out of hand."

He opened his mouth to speak, but there were no words. He wanted to say she had it wrong—had him wrong—but he wasn't sure he was right.

"Look, I've learned a lot about myself since we first met. I know me—know that my personality always made me the perfect 'other woman,' even when I was there first," she laughed sarcastically and shook her head. "I was always the girl willing to wait or share…take whatever attention I could get."

She looked up into his eyes. "And you were the guy who couldn't keep doing that to me. It didn't change who I was in the years that followed, and I didn't change who I was until I became the 'other woman' to a bottle of vodka. God found me at the bottom of that dark place, and I realized He was what I had been looking for all along. Sometimes, I forget that."

Her eyes turned back to her coffee cup. "So, I appreciate that you didn't want to put me in that position again, but knowing I'm still the nice girl you don't want to hurt… That still hurts."

It was McKay's turn to avoid eye contact. He sighed, staring off at the corner of his office, but seeing nothing. "Seems like I can't avoid hurting you no matter what I do."

She gave a half-hearted laugh. "What we could be is worth regretting; I have a right to feel that. But, my recent behavior notwithstanding, I'm not all that fragile. I'm a big girl, Chief. I don't bounce back immediately, but I bounce back…given time."

She rose to leave but stopped with her hand on the doorknob.

"Someday, being a lone wolf might get awfully lonely, Marcus…"

After she left, McKay moved to sit in his desk chair. He grabbed a stack of paperwork intent on putting everything out of his mind. After a moment, he folded his hands under his chin and gave in to the thoughts running through his head.

"It already is, Trilby. It already is."

The truth was he hadn't had a serious relationship since after he broke it off with Trilby years ago. They had met at a dark time in both their lives, had bonded, and loved too fast and too deep.

At first, she was a breath of fresh air, despite their sad circumstances. She believed the best of him and tried to build him up at every turn so he would see himself the way she saw him.

It wasn't her intense need for him that forced him to push her away in the end; he was used to being needed…and used. Instead, it was how overwhelmed he was by that vision of himself—by the expectations he put on himself to try to be the man she believed him to be.

She wanted to share herself *completely* with someone who would do the same; she deserved that. He chose another woman who fit his comfort zone, and, in the process, shattered Trilby's heart.

They remained friends, and he watched from a distance as she gave herself away to others who took advantage of her—still seeking the partner she needed. He had gone through a few long-term relationships before settling on less confining friendships. But now, he couldn't remember the last time he had even had a date—six, eight months? And he had felt more alive when Trilby kissed him than he had in years—some part of him coming awake again.

He rubbed his lips, feeling the electricity and passion she had left there. *Could he be the man she needed now?*

CHAPTER FOURTEEN

DAY NINE

Gwen opened her office door to find Trilby lying on the couch, her arm across her eyes.

"Ready for another bar brawl so soon?" The doctor hung her white coat up and lifted Trilby's head up just enough so she could scoot her lap under it.

"OK, pal, spill."

Trilby kept her eyes closed. "Why are you working, Gwen?"

"Because people like you need me. Talk."

Trilby had tried to keep her issue with McKay to herself the past few days. When she heard Gwen was back in the office, she drove over.

Trilby sighed. "More dreams."

"About Marcus?"

She felt tears roll out of Trilby's eyes and onto her cashmere skirt.

"Yep."

"That bad?"

"The dreams are horrible. But there's more."

"I see. Well, how about you sit up like a big girl, let me get you a tissue, and we'll talk about it?"

"I'd rather you get me a stiff drink."

"You and me both, sister." She pushed Trilby out of her lap with her good arm and handed over the box of tissues.

"A stiff drink will not fix that mess going on under your nose." She smiled. "And I do not advocate the other prescription before close of business on a workday."

Trilby wiped her nose and eyes. "Fine, but there better be a margarita at the end of all of this."

Gwen laughed. "Oh, Trilby, you know I have your back." She sat back, waiting while Trilby tried to figure out where to start. Silently, Trilby marveled at the fact that Gwen didn't so much as brush at the dark, wet spot on her expensive garment.

"So, you had a dream?"

"A couple. I told you about the first one—just a feeling of evil with Marcus. The next one, we were back at the house in New Mexico, and then he turned into a wisp of smoke and was gone."

Trilby paused in case Gwen had any great insights. Gwen raised a brow. "That's a pretty brief description. Nothing else important?"

Trilby sighed. "The usual sexual tension that leads to nothing. I hardly see where that's the point."

"If you say so. Please continue."

Trilby huffed. "Then, the other night, I dreamed that I followed the smoke into this giant creepy smile with corpses inside, and I knew more corpses were coming."

Now, Trilby was the one with an expectant look on her face.

"That must have been terrifying."

"And then some. I woke up so freaked out that I called Marcus."

"What did he have to say?"

"Nothing. I hung up."

Gwen just nodded, the eyebrow raised again.

"And then he showed up at my door."

Gwen's face finally registered a mild amount of surprise. "I see. And what happened?"

The tears were back. "Nothing. Everything. I don't know."

"Take a breath, Trilby, and just tell me what's going on."

"What's going on is I'm having crazy-lady dreams, and then I call Marcus in the middle of the night and freak him out, so he comes over, and because I'm a crazy lady, he winds up sleeping next to me to make me feel safe."

"And that's a problem? Him wanting you to feel safe?"

"No. Yes. I don't know. I kissed him!"

"Oh. I see. And that's the problem?"

"No." Trilby's voice became almost a whisper. "The problem is… My heart still wants what it shouldn't."

Gwen nodded. "So, you're frightened for Marcus, and he's protective of you, and in that circle of safety, you reached out for something…more?"

Trilby shrugged. "I guess."

"And he didn't want that?"

Trilby shook her head. "He said he doesn't want to hurt me."

"Well, I think that ship has sailed."

Trilby offered her a half-hearted smile.

"So, you're feeling…?"

"I don't know."

"Unwanted? Unloved? Homicidal? Stop me when I hit an adjective that sounds appropriate."

Trilby laughed. "Oh, no. I felt wanted. And I know he cares about me. And lucky for him, I'm sworn to serve and protect."

"So what then?"

104

Trilby sighed. "I want him to be…different."

"Ah. Well, we know what happens to women who try to change men…"

"Yeah, yeah… That's just it. I don't want him…*not* to be Marcus; I just want him to realize who Marcus already is and what he really needs."

"And you want that to be you?"

"It would be very convenient," Trilby smiled.

"OK, girl. Here's my prescription: It's a good time for a late lunch, so we're going to go get a plate of hot, fattening food at a good Mexican restaurant and do girl talk until you feel better, and then, you're going to go home and sleep."

"Margaritas?"

"I am officially calling this work day done." She stood to move to the intercom on her desk and let her receptionist know she was leaving for the day. "But first, you're going to need to change out of the uniform…and fix your face."

☐

"Marcus, sorry I didn't get back to you sooner. You said you already got the info you needed?" Fontane decided he had to make the call.

"Yeah. Yeah. It's turned into a real mess, Dave. We went out to Parker and met a doctor that worked at the camp. The long and short of it, he tried to kill one of our shrinks, and we had to take him down. Said Adam Carlton told him to do it."

Fontane hoped McKay didn't hear him swallow the lump in his throat.

"Earlier in the day, Dr. White gave us a ledger somebody kept of the boys they ran through that place—goes back decades, way before the doctor was ever there…as a doctor. It's complicated. Anyway, we're combing through it, but things are out of hand."

A ledger? Fontane knew his father had gone to great lengths to hide his son's identity when he left him in that hellhole, but not knowing who had kept the ledger or what was in it made him nervous. *Is there a trail back to me after all?*

"Sounds like you could use some help."

"And some big-boy connections, Dave. I think it's about time I got the feds involved. I've got psychos coming out of the woodwork out here."

"I'll see you tomorrow afternoon, McKay."

"Thanks, Dave."

Fontane hung up the phone and pounded the top of his desk. Adam had turned White and taken down Kevin, Casey and Jeff; Fontane was sure he was in the crosshairs—not of the investigation…yet…but of some nefarious plot coming out of his past to haunt him. He needed to get ahead of this thing, and fast.

Cold determination settled across his features as he turned toward his computer keyboard. "Time to find Adam."

CHAPTER FIFTEEN

DAY NINE, EVENING

"Working late?"

McKay looked up at the knock on his office door. "Dave, hey! Come in. We're all working around the clock these days." He rose and moved to shake Fontane's hand. "Thanks for coming."

"Have to admit, Marcus, your case has me intrigued—the boys from Carlton Camp. Fill me in and tell me what you need."

"I tell you, Dave, I'm not even sure. Ever since we found the photo of them, the case has gone off-the-rails crazy."

Fontane flinched inwardly, but his face betrayed no emotion. "A photo?"

McKay indicated for Fontane to sit and moved back behind his desk.

"From when they were kids in the camp; first names were listed on the back—five boys. All but one has been identified."

"And the others are all dead…?"

McKay nodded as he sipped his coffee. "All four turned feral, for lack of a better word—suddenly violent and totally out of character. The first three were taken down before they could do any serious harm… physically."

Fontane nodded. He knew all too well the meaning of

psychological pain. "And the last?"

"Donald Carter. Took a bank president hostage, killed him in what looks to be a murder-suicide."

"Wow. And you guys have no motive for the events?"

"Nope. And no reason for their change in behavior. Carter was the only one with anything in his system. He'd been drinking heavily for a couple of months according to friends and family, so it wasn't surprising that his alcohol level was sky-high. But the others were clean. And I don't even know where to start with the doctor."

"Ok. So what's your theory on the boys in the photo first?" Fontane appeared calm, showing only a professional interest. Hiding his true thoughts had long ago become second nature.

"All we've got right now are four dead guys with ties to the same boot camp—a camp with a sordid history. A crabby old guy told us some ghost stories and sent us after Elsa Cooke. That put is in contact with Stephen White. We didn't get any specifics, but he confirmed that there was a lot wrong with how the boys were treated in the camp. I'm inclined to lean toward some kind of programming through torture—something that 'turned' these guys after years of living normal, quiet lives."

Fontane nodded his head as if deeply considering the concept, his face remained placid despite the cacophony of alarm bells sounding through his brain.

"So this Dr. White confirmed the abuse at the camp, and you're thinking it was all done with some plan in mind? That's quite a theory. Who's your suspect?"

"My money's on Adam Carlton. He helped run the place toward the end, before the foreclosure, and just before they were evicted, he killed his father in a very public and very grisly manner, then disappeared. Not a blip on the radar since."

Again, Fontane nodded. "What's the motive? The first three were purely domestic, right?"

"The first two seem so. The third may have had some reason to go after the Sheriff of Chickasaw County."

"The Sheriff?"

"He asked for the sheriff when SWAT approached, told them the sheriff had to pay. We haven't found any connection yet, other than the sheriff was part of the raid that closed the camp."

"Ah. And the banker?"

"Held the loan on the camp. When Marvin Carlton couldn't make his payments, and the bank began foreclosure, he was set to lose his family's home, too—one that had been in his family for three generations. Of course, he was dead before that happened."

"So, who's the other hit? And how did Adam Carlton manage to set up such an elaborate plan so long ago?"

"That part has us stumped, Dave. How could he have programmed them to play their parts years after the fact? Act out specific orders? That's beyond me."

Just then, Trilby raced past McKay's open door, glancing in as she did and locking eyes with Fontane.

With a curious look on his face, McKay said, "But one of my best officers is following a hunch, and her gut is rarely wrong."

Carlsen's head appeared in the doorway. "Baines is headed to another scene—apparent murder-suicide. Told me to grab you on my way."

McKay snatched his jacket and hat off the coat rack as he headed toward the door. "Maybe number five is already making his appearance. Shall we?"

Fontane shook his head. "You go ahead. I'll try to catch up. My superior wanted a briefing ASAP to see what resources we can get in here, so I need to get a hotel room and set up shop."

McKay seemed surprised but nodded as he went through the door. Looking over his shoulder, he said, "Ok, we'll catch up later. I'll meet you at O'Malley's."

Fontane smiled. "Sounds like a plan. Text me when you get there."

☐

As McKay pulled up to the crime scene tape, he took note of the crowd gathered behind it and the houses along the small cul de sac. So far, the neighborhood wasn't in keeping with the last four cases.

Walking up the sidewalk, he faced the front of a low-income housing unit. No. 211 was taped off, the door standing open for the evidence techs and the M.E. The neighbors—a young woman he knew from a prostitution sting six months prior and her toddler—stood on the porch next door watching his officers.

Inside the front door, the smell of cigarettes and booze assailed his senses. The place was filthy, the furniture in disarray. Trilby and Carlsen stood with the other officers against the far wall of the living room waiting. Daniel and the crime scene techs were arranged along the other.

Marcus made his way to Trilby. "What gives?"

It was Carlsen who answered. "Pair of dogs guarding the body. We can't get in until animal control can get them out. They're about five minutes out."

"I see. Ok. Fill me in."

"Another murder-suicide, as far as we can tell. We'll know

more when we get in there. Neighbor heard arguing and gunshots. We can see the bodies through the window in almost the same positions as the Carter case."

"So, any idea who our players are?"

Guy who lives here is Kirk Kane. Neighbor says he was a good guy with some bad habits."

"Aren't they all?"

"She says she was here when the shooter arrived. They were all partying, but she had to go put the baby to bed."

"Mother of the year…"

"Yeah, well, she was trying to get the kid to sleep when she heard the yelling and the gunshots. She called the cops."

"She have a name for her new friend?"

"She only heard Kane call him Michael."

"Kirk and Michael? Neither of those is a name on the photo…" McKay looked from Carlsen to Trilby for confirmation.

She shook her head. "Nope."

"So, you're thinking it's tied to the other cases because the MO. for the kill is the same?"

"That and Chelsea from next door—who has given up her previous profession and is going back to school in case you wondered… Chelsea said Kane told her Mike was like a brother to him because they had both lived through something terrible at some camp they went to."

While they were talking, animal control arrived and entered the bedroom. After much commotion, they came out with two visibly shaken white pit bulls on leashes. McKay gave the leader a questioning nod to ask if the room was clear.

"All yours, Chief. These guys were just trying to keep their master safe." She reached down to pet the dog she handled. "They're more scared of you guys than you are of them, I think."

One of the officers behind her disagreed. "You didn't see them when we first opened that door! Nothing but teeth coming at me!"

"I know, Bob. You did the right thing calling us so no one—you or them—got hurt. We'll take these guys in and get them checked out. I'm betting they'll get a good new home, though."

McKay stopped to let the nearest dog smell his hand, waiting until the terrified pup nudged his fingers before he gently swept his hand over the dog's brow. "He's a beauty."

"And loyal to a fault. Whoever that man is, he took good care of these guys because they would have done anything for him."

McKay looked up into his officer's eyes, contemplating. "It's true, I suppose, that you can tell a lot about a person by how he treats his dog."

☐

Inside the next room, a familiar sight waited. McKay agreed the positioning of the bodies—the duct-taped hands and feet, the way the killer's body fell over his victim, the pistol nearby—was a dead match to the Carter scene. Only the upper-middle-class ambiance was missing.

Daniel was rolling the first body as McKay stepped closer. "Anything of note, Doc?"

"If you're thinking it's a lot like the Carter case, I'd have to say at first blush that you're right. I've got an ID here for the shooter: Michael Monahans." He handed the wallet and ID to McKay.

"I see he's got a little more middle-class address. Carlsen, take a couple of uniforms, get over there and make sure—"

"He didn't leave a dead family in his wake?" Trilby finished McKay's thought for him.

As Daniel's assistant bagged the body of Michael Monahans, the M.E. began his cursory exam of Kirk Kane. He handed the wallet to McKay.

"Not much in here. A few bucks… And the business card for a lawyer…"

He handed the card to Trilby. "I know this guy. A real ambulance-chaser. Wonder what Kane was doing with a guy like that?"

Daniel rose from his exam of Kane's body. "Nothing else stands out to me here. I'll get them back to the morgue and let you know something ASAP."

"Thanks, doll." Trilby nodded in his direction before turning back to the scene. McKay hung back to let her work the room in her logical way. He watched her as she made a meticulous lap of the room, her brow furrowed in concentration until she came back to stand next to him again.

"Looks pretty cut and dried on this end of things—murder-suicide, just like Carter. We need to get back and check that ledger from the camp, see when these guys were there in relation to our mysterious five, look for a motive for this event that makes sense in relation to the camp, if any."

McKay nodded. "David Fontane, my FBI contact, was in my office when you sent Carlsen after me. He doesn't have anything more on the camp, but I'm meeting him for a beer later, and I'll see what he thinks about this turn of events. I've asked for FBI assistance on this; we're in over our heads."

Trilby nodded and turned to leave. McKay's hand on her arm

restrained her. "Are you ok?"

She looked over her shoulder and back at the scene, then nodded. The sadness in her eyes cut McKay to the core. He turned back to the room, not wanting to watch her walk away.

CHAPTER SIXTEEN

McKay wasn't surprised to find Trilby standing beside the body of Kirk Kane as Daniel examined him in the morgue. He hadn't seen her since she left the scene and had come looking for a report on any findings Daniel had for Kane and Monahans.

"Why, Marcus, what a delight!" Daniel managed to project the image of a perfect host despite the gore staining his gloved hands, and the gruesome site stretched out in front of him. "I simply never see enough of you, sir."

Marcus kept his distance. He wasn't interested in suiting up and didn't want to walk out of the morgue with anyone else's bodily fluids on his nice clean uniform.

"Daniel, Trilby," he said by way of greeting. "Got anything?"

"Well, similarities first… A number of old injuries that *could* have been inflicted by a third party or could be childhood accidents; otherwise unremarkable physical exam." He stripped his gloves off and moved to stand near McKay. "Unlike the first three subjects, Mr. Kane and Mr. Monahans had both alcohol and marijuana in their systems, as expected from the scene."

"So, as unremarkable as the other four then?"

"Yes, I'm afraid so."

She removed her gloves and gown and moved toward the exit. "I have a bit more upstairs. Thanks, Daniel."

"Always, my lovely."

McKay looked to Daniel before following. "Thanks, Daniel. I appreciate you jumping into this tonight. The faster we get results, the faster we can figure things out."

"Of course, Marcus. Always happy to help."

☐

The elevator ride up to the squad room was an exercise in pure silence. McKay found himself wishing for the horrible Muzak played in his doctor's office.

As they exited, Trilby grabbed her coffee cup off her desk to refill it, and McKay did the same, meeting her in the war room. She stuck photos of Kane and Monahans on the white board. McKay took a seat opposite the board, and Trilby stood in front of it.

"Canvas didn't turn up much at Kane's place past what we got from Chelsea—good guy who found himself in a bad place. Seems he talked a lot about the abuse he endured at the camp, blamed everything bad in his life on that stretch of circumstances."

"And Monahans?"

"He was a computer programmer—middle class; wife and kids; quiet guy—"

"Kept to himself mostly… Yeah, I get it." He tried a smile, but she didn't return it.

"There aren't five names corresponding with the photo listed in the same month as Kane and Monahans. I poured over the ledger, and I only see a period of about six months where five boys of about the right ages and names were at the camp at the same time. Most of them were gone before Kane and Monahans arrived. One overlapped for a few months—Dave, no last name—he was there more than two years."

"That long?"

"Like someone left him there and forgot about him. He left a couple months before the place shut down. Whoever kept the ledger gets sloppy during that time, and it finally slacks off altogether about two weeks before Carlton Sr. is found."

"This case gets weirder by the moment." McKay rose to stand at the board, staring at the photo of the boys.

"There's more. We were able to get hold of the lawyer from the card Kane was carrying. Turns out he was suing Chickasaw County over his time at Carlton Camp. Lawyer said Kane had gone straight from the camp to the Sheriff's Department trying to get the camp closed down, and that he was as terrorized by ex-campmates *after* the camp closed as he had been while it was open."

"Like the good doctor told us… What happened there was something none of them wanted anyone else to know about. So what was his actual claim?"

"Kane was suing the Chickasaw County Sheriff for leaking Kane's part in the investigation. If the lawsuit moved forward, *lots* of people would have known their secrets, so maybe that's what pushed Monahans over the edge."

Trilby took a seat at the far end of the table—away from McKay. "A waste really, since the leak sent Adam Carlton on his rampage, and the county wound up with plenty of reasons—and the help of the FBI director, no less—to go in and shut the camp down."

"A slaughtered body hung out for public consumption did the trick all right." He took a long, contemplative sip of coffee. "So, you think this is a coincidence? That this thing with Kane and Monahans just happened to come up as the other plot was underway?"

"I don't believe in coincidence, but I've got no proof of a plot either way. Still, I figure someone—probably Adam Carlton—was unhappy the camp was closed and is coming back to punish the people he feels were responsible."

She looked at her watch; well past 9 p.m. "I'm beat. We can get a fresh perspective tomorrow."

McKay nodded as she headed for the door. "I'll catch up with Fontane in a bit and ask him if he has any leads on Carlton. Good night, Trilby. Sleep well."

He was not surprised that she didn't answer; she'd come around in her own time. He hoped.

□

Trilby swept her case files off her desk into an unruly stack and headed toward the parking lot. She wanted out of the building and out of her uniform, but she knew there was no way she would be sleeping anytime soon.

Walking out to her patrol car, she had the sensation she was being watched. She turned to look behind her, but the two patrolmen smoking at the station entrance were uninterested in her, and she couldn't make out anyone else in the vicinity. She kept her awareness up as she unlocked her car and slid inside, then watched for any tail as she headed home. She saw nothing, but that didn't keep the hair on the back of her neck from standing out.

She pulled into her driveway, collected her files in one arm and left her gun hand free. She set the files down while she opened the front door, turning so she faced the side and could see her yard.

Scooping up her files, she hurried inside and bolted the door.

"You're being silly, Trilby. Paranoid."

Still, after she undressed, she came back to the kitchen with the Sig in hand. Something told her to keep it close. She warmed up dinner but denied herself the wine in favor of sharp alertness. She jumped when her phone rang, spilling iced tea down the front of her T-shirt.

"Baines," she growled.

"Trilby? Everything ok?"

"Hey, Doc." Trilby wasn't sure she had the energy for a conversation with Gwen. "I'm fine. Just a little jumpy and wet."

"Wet? OK. I was just checking in."

"I'm getting by."

"And not in the mood to talk about it. OK. You know where I am."

"I do, Gwen. Thanks."

Trilby headed back to the bedroom to change, opting for a sweatshirt this time after the cold iced tea. She took the Sig, the files and her laptop into the living room. After an hour of sifting through her notes, Trilby was no closer to new leads—or sleep—than she had been when she started.

She dialed McKay's cell phone, and he answered on the second ring. Bar noise filled the background.

"Trilby? What's up?"

"Did you get anything from Fontane?"

"He isn't here yet. Told me to meet him, but it's been almost an hour. Starting to think I've been stood up. I'm gonna bail and try to catch up to him in the morning."

"Oh. OK. Well, I'll see you tomorrow then."

"Sure thing. Goodnight, Trilby."

"Goodnight."

Disappointed that Fontane hadn't panned out with new leads, she left the files on her coffee table and took the Sig to her front windows, peeking out through closed blinds. She couldn't shake the feeling someone was out there, but if it were true, they were as invisible as a wisp of smoke.

"Something's coming, Lord. I don't know what it is, but I feel it. Things are about to get very, very dark."

CHAPTER SEVENTEEN

DAY NINE, LATE EVENING

If anyone could say he knew Adam Carlton, it was David Fontane. He had been Adam's favorite pupil at the camp, learning from him and emulating him in every way. If Adam were within 100 miles of Willow Creek, Fontane would find him.

He had come to Willow Creek after tracking Adam's various aliases. He should have known Adam would be close to the action. Fontane checked the maps app on his phone for area hotels, choosing the most luxurious. Adam would be there, renting out a suite in its most secluded section. Fontane turned his unmarked vehicle toward the Grant Hotel downtown.

As Fontane approached the front desk, he noted the young, handsome bellboy waiting nearby. *Adam would love you.* Fontane flashed his FBI ID and was rewarded with the knowledge that a reclusive and somewhat odd man named Albert Carl Holmes had taken up residence in the penthouse suite. The description matched an older version of the Adam in Fontane's mind.

As Fontane turned toward the elevators, he smiled, enjoying the private joke with Adam—"Albert" he corrected himself—who had shared his favorite books with Fontane, as well.

The elevator doors opened onto a short, brightly lit hallway that featured a large vase of lilies beside one of two doors. Fontane had no doubt that this was the current home of Adam Carlton; the other door led to a stairwell.

Why are you nervous? Fontane couldn't get past the twist in his gut. It had been years since he had seen Adam—and he had hoped never to see him again. It wasn't that he held any animosity toward Adam, rather he knew how easily Adam's dark personality could consume his own.

He stood a long while in front of the plain white door before he finally knocked. There was an even longer pause before the door slowly opened.

Even with the description from downstairs, Fontane was not prepared to see the years displayed on Adam's face, and it oddly pained him. Adam nodded and stepped back with a sweep of his arm to invite Fontane into the suite.

"Did you expect me?" Fontane's eyes took in every detail of Adam's appearance—no weapons—and looked for any threats, as well as exits, in the room. He kept Adam in his peripheral vision as he walked to the far side of a beautifully appointed living area. To others, he might look like a kindly old man, but Fontane knew him to be a lethal and remorseless killer. Even *old* rattlesnakes were to be feared…

"Expect? David, I have never been able to *expect* anything of you." Adam chuckled. He sat in an overstuffed leather chair and indicated the opposite sofa to Fontane.

"Let's not play games, Adam." Fontane sat on the edge of the sofa cushion, ready to move suddenly if necessary. He hadn't felt so anxious—and yet so alive—in a very long time.

"Carl, please. Adam Carlton is no more."

Fontane nodded. "As you wish. Carl, then. What are you playing at, *Carl*?"

Adam smiled. "I take it you mean your friends?"

"Not my friends, but yes, the others. All gone. And you're up to something. What are you doing?"

Adam lifted his hands in front of him palms up as he shrugged his shoulders. "I haven't done anything …"

"Don't feed me your semantics. You and I both know the seeds you planted in those men."

"*You and I* planted those seeds."

"I'm not part of this revenge plot—or whatever it is. And you've planted no seeds in me. *"*

"Of course not." Adam waved the notion away as if it disgusted him. "You were never *programmed* for your part in the plan. However, now that things have become…complicated. You *are* in a…delicate position."

There it is. He thinks he's got me. Fontane leaned back into the plush sofa, at ease now that he knew Adam's strategy was not physical.

"Delicate?"

"The son of George Fontane; well-respected FBI agent; it wouldn't do for people to find out who you *really* are."

"I see." Fontane leaned forward again, bracing his elbows on his knees. He wasn't surprised that Adam knew who he was, or that he had kept track of him. *But how long has he known? Is it in the ledger?*

"And you are prepared to tell people who I am?"

"Me? Heaven's no. Why would I draw attention to myself?"

Adam rose and walked to the bar behind Fontane, who turned to keep him in sight. "Drink?"

"No. I'm good."

Adam smiled, turning back to pour himself a brandy. "Well, really, that's a matter of opinion, I suppose."

He returned to his seat, ignoring the fury in Fontane's eyes. "You know I prefer the shadows, Fontane, but I have friends who *love* to tell stories."

Fontane nodded. He had waited a long time for the other shoe to drop, wondering what price Adam would exact for his silence. "And what if I just kill you right here and now and be done with it?"

"I suspect my little bellboy friend in the hall and the lovely woman at the front desk who sent you up here would know exactly who to point to when my body was discovered."

Fontane laughed. "Do you honestly believe your body would be found?"

Adam took another long sip. "Oh, probably not. I taught you well, and I'm sure you've honed your skills in the years since, but really…so much trouble, so much risk."

He set his drink aside and opened his palms before him. "It seems unless we come to some agreement, either tonight will end badly for one of us, or we will both be looking over our shoulder for a while."

"At least until you're dead." Fontane's smile was ice-cold.

Adam laughed. "Yes. Well, until *one* of us is dead. Or…"

"Of course. My part in your little plan."

Adam smiled slyly. "Would the world be so much better with one of us not in it?"

"Probably. What do you want from me, *Carl*?"

The feral smile returned. "Nothing you haven't done before, David dear. But fret not about your part in the plan. I'm afraid that ship has sailed. Once you complete the task at hand, you may well be…out of position to assist me further."

Adam's voice was pure-spun silk sliding across Fontane's psyche. As much as he wanted to keep his distance—both literally and psychologically—he felt himself sliding into his old skin.

"I'm not who I was before." His protest was weak, and Adam brushed it aside with a wave of his hand.

"Don't be silly, David. People like us never change."

Fontane shook his head, as much to clear it as to negate the words coming out of Adam's mouth. "I'm an FBI agent; decorated; venerated. Not to mention I'm right in the middle of your mess already with the local cops."

"Yes, the local police force has been more…thorough than I anticipated from such a small town." Adam rose to look at the darkening sky beyond glass doors leading to the balcony. "But then, there was no Marcus McKay when the foundations of my plan were laid. It is fortunate, I suppose, that he chose you as his FBI contact…"

"For now, but he's a good cop with good cops working for him."

Another wave of Adam's hand. "They will all fall apart without the esteemed *Chief* McKay."

"You underestimate Baines."

"Ah, the lovely redhead, no? What is her name? Something musical…Oh, *Trilby!* You know, I looked it up. Someone gave her the name of a great literary heroine. Isn't that funny?

"Yes, she was this spritely half-Irish artist's model with a beastly inability to sing. *Svengali* transformed her into a great operatic diva by mystical control."

Fontane was unimpressed. "Do you have a point, Carl?"

"Well, perhaps our pet policewoman is no less in the control of her master, McKay. I'll wager her ties to him are stronger than any of them. She'll shatter when he's…gone. But, regardless, I will handle Trilby Baines."

Fontane doubted that scenario. "Even if I agreed with your analysis of the situation, what is it you propose we do?"

Adam turned back to Fontane. "We? As I said, McKay is no part of my plan. He's all yours."

"Mine? You brought this on yourself, *Carl*. Why should I—"

Adam cut him off. "What choice do you have, David? You and I both know perfectly well why you're here. Why make this pretense?"

"I'm here to find out what crazy plot you're playing out and what it has to do with me. Why should I take on this risk for your foolish behavior?"

"Foolish!" Adam howled with sudden rage. "I did it for you— for us—to get even with them, to get you back!"

Fontane stared at Adam, dumbstruck.

"Back? What are you talking about, Adam?" Fontane said, giving up on the pretense of Adam's new identity.

"I knew…if they started dying… I knew you'd come. You'd find me. I wanted to help you find yourself again." Adam's words trailed off at the end. "And then we'd finish it."

"Finish it?"

"The plan, David. The last part of the plan. You would finish the plan, and we would disappear. But it's ruined…"

Adam's eyes hardened, and his voice grew dark. "All ruined by the chief and that...*woman*."

"What was I supposed to do, Adam? Take care of McKay? How could you have known—?"

"That I would need you to take care of the police chief? I didn't, and that was not the part I intended you to play. The local police played no part in taking down our home. But the FBI..."

"The FBI?"

"The director himself," Adam said, staring out into the night sky once again.

"How could you have known—?"

"Don't be foolish, David. Don't you think I *knew* who you were? Who your father was? I knew long before you did what destiny he had in mind for you, and I made sure you followed it."

"You knew? Adam, they have a ledger, did you—"

"Don't be a fool, David." Adam spat out the words. "I left no trail back to you."

Fontane wanted to walk away from the whole crazy mess. No. He wanted to kill this crazy old man and disappear. But he could see no way to make either happen.

"It doesn't matter now. What matters is that you and I can live in a state of détente. We can survive—apart—both unwilling to expose the other at our own expense. But if McKay finds out about you, everything you have become is gone like a puff of smoke."

☐

Fontane left the hotel under a dark cloud. Adam—Carl was right. Fontane couldn't kill Carl, not until he was sure no more loose ends were waiting to catch him up in his past, and he couldn't trust that Adam had swept away any clues to his identity.

That left McKay and his department. Fontane needed to know how close they were, and who knew too much… He checked his watch, even angrier when he saw how much time he had wasted with Carl. As he waited for the valet to bring his car around, he began to formulate a plan. *If McKay is still waiting…*

Arriving at the pub in record time, he parked his car down the street and hoofed it to the entrance just in time to catch McKay making his exit.

"Marcus!"

McKay turned but didn't smile. "Hey, Dave. I was beginning to think you stood me up."

"So sorry, man. I got caught up in something—you know how it is."

McKay had to admit he had more than once left a buddy—or a date—waiting because duty called. "Sure thing." He pointed to the entrance behind him. "Did you want to go back in?"

Fontane could hear the noise inside. He needed to get McKay somewhere quiet to talk, but not alert him that anything was wrong.

"Hey, maybe we could grab a fifth and take it back to my place? After the week I've had, I'd kind of prefer a little more…quiet."

McKay nodded. "A man after my own heart. I was feeling really *old* in there." He nodded down the street toward his car. "I'm down this way."

Fontane indicated behind him. "I'm over here. Follow me?"

"Sounds like a plan."

☐

McKay climbed into the driver's seat of his 1978 Datsun 280Z and turned the key. He smiled. He didn't drive his toy as often as he should. He had worked like a dog to buy the car when he was 18 and kept it purring like a kitten all these years. It was the Black Pearl Edition and still shined like it was rolling off the showroom floor.

He made a U-turn and pulled up behind Fontane's unmarked unit, following him out of downtown and toward the highway motels with one stop at a liquor store along the way.

McKay thought of calling Trilby to let her know Fontane had finally shown up, maybe he'd be able to spark some new lead out of him with what they had learned today. Looking at the time—nearly midnight—he decided better of it. Hopefully, she was sleeping.

He tried not to picture her curled up peacefully in her bed…and failed. *McKay, you're a fool. You should have never pushed her away the first time, and if you do it again, you deserve the life you get.*

☐

Trilby may have been in her nice, warm bed, but she was far from peaceful. Another dream had her in its clutches, and she writhed and screamed trying to break free.

The gaping smoke smile was back, gobbling up McKay and swallowing her whole behind him. The bodies were clearer now—boys, their mouths gagged, their hands tied, unable to escape or cry out. She tried to step over them, running after McKay's disappearing form. He was following someone.

McKay! Wait! No! It's a trap!

If he heard her, he showed no sign. She'd never reach him at this pace, gingerly picking her way around the bodies. She took her eyes off them. *They aren't real, Trilby. Get to Marcus.*

She ran. She didn't look down, didn't look anywhere but straight ahead—only at McKay's back—and she gained on him. As she reached out to grab him, she saw the man he chased. She knew that face…

McKay turned to her. *Trilby?*

Marcus, stop. Stay with me.

He looked back to the man running from him—running toward the darkness.

Stop, David! You can't…

Trilby sprang awake, sitting upright in the pitch black. She snatched at the bedside table, desperate to find her phone. Premonition or not, she wanted to know where Marcus was and that David Fontane was nowhere near him.

☐

"It's a puzzler, Dave." McKay lounged on the sofa in Fontane's room, a glass of Jameson in his hand. Fontane, opting for a T-shirt and jeans over his suit, sat in the opposite chair. It was a cozy suite with a view of the pool below.

McKay had filled Fontane in on the details of the case, and in return, Fontane gave more details on his pretense of help from the Bureau. More agents were to arrive in the morning, he lied, and a task force would be put in place.

"Well, Trilby will be less than thrilled, but I don't see us getting anywhere on this as fast as we need to." McKay sipped at the Irish whiskey. "I've got good guys, but this is too much."

Fontane nodded, sipping at his glass as well. He had poured them both a drink as soon as they arrived, and waited patiently for the drug to take effect. Poor McKay, he never suspected Fontane would drug him, much less what would come next.

Fontane had looked down into his own glass, studying the swirling liquor as he listened to McKay's speech slur. He heard the glass drop and shatter and nodded once to himself before he rose from the chair. Back to business. It wasn't business Fontane would enjoy—at least he didn't think so. He liked McKay, maybe he would have even considered him a friend, if Fontane had friends.

He checked McKay's pulse. Slow, but steady, as was his breathing. *Well, he'll get a good bit of rest on the way there.*

Fontane had turned toward the bathroom when he heard McKay's phone go off. The sound made him jump, and he snatched at McKay's coat on the arm of the sofa.

Trilby. He sighed. She was *Carl's* problem…for now.

Fontane got McKay to his feet. He topped McKay's modest height by about three inches, but it was still a monumental task to drag him down the hallway and three flights of stairs to the exit near Fontane's car. Just to be sure, he loaded McKay into the trunk—of his own car.

As he made the drive to Parker, Fontane thought about the strange turns his life had taken. If he had never been sent to Carlton Camp… If he had never met Adam… *What? Would you be someone else, David?*

It disturbed him to hear Adam's voice in his head now—just as he had over all these years since he left the camp.

I didn't make you who you are, David. I refined you. I taught you how to be the best version of your monstrous self.

"Shut up, Adam! You don't know me!"

He heard laughter echo in his mind. *David dear, no one knows you better.*

CHAPTER EIGHTEEN

DAY NINE, LATE NIGHT

The phone rang unanswered, and Trilby's mind flew to a thousand dark possibilities. Her next call was to dispatch, where a surprised officer took down the information for an APB on the chief and an FBI agent.

"Trilby. What's up?" Carlsen was off-duty, but he answered on the first ring, just as she knew he would.

"Mike, I've got a feeling something's wrong with the chief. I called his cell, no answer, and that's not like him." She wasn't going to tell Carlsen about her crazy dream.

"Any idea where he is?"

"He's with that FBI agent, Fontane; they were supposed to meet for a drink. Mike, I don't trust that guy. I called a friend at the Bureau; he said Fontane is supposed to be on leave." She paused to give Carlsen a chance to process.

"So, maybe he's here as a friend of the chief?"

"Except, he told the chief the Bureau was taking over, so I had my friend check the GPS tracker on his unmarked vehicle."

"And what did you get?"

"He went from the department to a motel on the outskirts of town and then to the Grant Hotel downtown."

Carlsen whistled. "Fancy digs."

"Yeah, and not where he's staying, so he must have been meeting someone. From there, he headed over to O'Malley's…"

"To meet the chief…"

"Right. When I spoke to McKay, he said he had already waited an hour on Fontane, but when Fontane got there, he left almost immediately and went back to his motel. My guess is he and the chief decided to have a quiet drink in Fontane's room instead, where they could talk. Fontane's car hasn't moved since, but my gut says something's up."

"He's driving an unmarked, flashing his badge. It's not like he's hiding, Trilby."

"I thought that, too, but now I'm guessing either he's not thinking straight, or he's just that confident that no one will suspect anything. Mike, I need you to check on his motel."

"Sure, Trilby. I'll meet you there in ten."

"Actually, I'm on my way to Parker."

"The camp? Why? You think he's tied to Carlton?"

"I don't know, Mike, but something… I just know Fontane has Marcus, and I have to get to Parker before—"

"Ok, Trilby, just slow down. Don't go charging into anything blind; I know you trust your gut, but there's no reason to go off half-cocked. I'll check on Fontane's motel and send a unit to McKay's house—"

"I already did. No McKay and his car is gone."

Trilby heard the sharp intake of breath on Carlsen's end of the call. They both knew the 280Z didn't move without McKay behind the wheel.

"Ok, Trilby. I'm calling for a Sheriff's deputy to meet you, just in case. Until then, keep back and stay low. I'll check the motel, and if anything looks out of place, I'll be headed your way with a SWAT team in tow. If you hear or see anything—"

"You'll be the first to know."

☐

Fontane dropped McKay unceremoniously in the middle of the barn. The man landed with a solid thud but didn't move. Fontane kicked him once to be sure, then turned to survey the decay around him. *What had become of his nest?* It sickened him to see it all falling apart, the years stealing away at the physical manifestation of memories he could not escape.

He heard groaning behind him. *No time to reminisce.* He was glad he had grabbed the rope from the trunk of his car before leaving the hotel. He retrieved it and looped it around both of McKay's wrists. Using the roof beam, he dragged the semi-conscious man to his feet and tied off the rope to leave him hanging there. He grabbed a bottle of water from the trunk and poured it over McKay's upturned face until the man choked and gasped awake.

"There he is! Sorry to wake you so rudely, but I need to be sure I know everything you know before I…dispatch you."

"Dispatch me? What is this, a bad Bond movie?"

Fontane smiled. "A sense of humor in the face of death; admirable, Marcus, but unwarranted. Make it easy on yourself. Tell me what I want to know, and I'll kill you quickly."

McKay took in his surroundings, confusion showing in his eyes.

"Don't you recognize it, Marcus? Or did you not get a chance to see all of Adam's little playground?"

Understanding turned to anger in an instant. "So, you're 'Dave' from the photo…One of the Fatherless Five?"

Fontane remained stoic.

"I've heard all about your little club," McKay said, looking around. "I take it this is the clubhouse?"

He leveled a steely gaze on Fontane. "You get your kicks from causing people pain. Why would I believe you'd treat me differently?"

"I'm not like that, Marcus. I was a victim, and I rose above it."

McKay spat out a laugh filled with disdain. "I see it in your eyes, Fontane. You're no victim."

Fontane took a step closer, his breath hot on McKay's cheek. "Very well, Marcus. Shall we play?"

Trilby raced toward Parker. She was 20 minutes out, and the deputy was on the other side of the county—35 minutes away.

Trilby's radio squawked. "Baines."

"Switch to Tac 10."

Trilby changed the radio settings to a lesser used tactical channel. "Go, Mike."

"SWAT en route, be there in 40." Carlsen sounded winded as he rushed to gather his gear and coordinate with his men. "We searched the hotel. Two used glasses, the chief's jacket and his cell phone were in Fontane's room. No sign of the chief or Fontane and the chief's car is nowhere to be seen."

Clumsy, Fontane. All of this is clumsy like you want to get caught. Trilby shook her head. *Delusional. He thinks he's in the clear—that we won't suspect him, won't figure it out.*

"He thinks he'll get away with it…"

"What?"

"Nothing," she said, snapping back at the sound of Carlsen's voice. "What about the Grant?"

"Nada. Front desk remembered him asking about the guy in the penthouse suite. Said he met with the guy—and older man, tall, seemed important. Guy signed in as Carl Holmes but stuck to his room. The clerk said Holmes took a liking to one of the bellboys, and we're looking for him to see what he knows."

How could we not have figured it out sooner? Not seen his name in the ledger? Something. Something should have told me before Marcus was in danger. If anything happens to him...

Her phone rang, and she snatched it up. "Marcus?"

"Trilby, it's Gwen."

Trilby took a deep breath. "Gwen, I can't talk right now. Why are you calling anyway?"

"Because Mike told me what's going on. Where are you?"

"Almost to Parker. Fontane's got him in that run-down boot camp. I've got to get there before he kills Marcus and disappears."

"Kills him? Are you sure that's what's happening, Trilby? You don't even know that's where they are."

"Then where is he, Gwen? My gut is telling me I need to get to Parker and fast. I just know, Gwen. He's one of Carlton's 'boys,' and he's got Marcus in…that place—his place, where he became the monster that he is. I've got to get to him."

"Well, telling you to wait on the cavalry would be pointless. So, here's what we're going to do. You're going to leave the line open on this call. You leave me here on the phone listening, and I'll relay whatever I hear back to the team on the way since you'll be in radio-silence. I've got a second phone here, and I'll open that line with Mike."

"Why do you have— Never mind. That sounds like a plan, I guess. Whatever will stop you talking so I can get in there and find Marcus."

"I take it that means you have arrived."

"I'm parked on the road out front. I put the phone on speaker, so don't talk after this, but the phone is on a clip on my belt. Can you hear?"

"Crystal, so far."

"Good. Now shush. I'm headed in."

"Headed where?"

"*Gwen…*"

"Last time, promise."

Trilby realized the question was a good one. She looked around the dilapidated property. She listened so intently, she thought her ears would bleed. Nothing. No movement. No sound. Then, she thought she saw the barest flicker of light from the direction of the barn. Her gut kicked her. *There.*

"Barn. Shut up. I'm headed in."

☐

Fontane stared at McKay's bleeding face. He'd long since given up trying to move the stubborn man with his fists. In his hand, a razor-sharp knife gleamed.

McKay spat blood in Fontane's eyes. "They will find you. You will pay for your crimes."

"Marcus, don't be a fool. No one suspects me, and no one is going to come looking for you here, now. When they—correction, when *we*—find your body tomorrow, they will assume some other crazy camp boy grew up to avenge dear old Adam."

Fontane ran the blade across McKay's abdomen, drawing a bright red line on the crisp, white shirt. McKay grimaced, his body going taut with pain.

"That is nothing compared to what's coming, Marcus. Answer my questions. How much does the redhead know? Is there anything besides the ledger that will send her looking for me?"

McKay's face hardened. The fire in his voice was palpable. "Do not touch Trilby." He accentuated every word.

Fontane laughed. "I don't intend to touch her… Unless Adam fails, of course."

McKay started. "Where is she? Have you done something?"

"Don't be silly. I told you, she's Adam's problem. I haven't got a clue where she is right now."

McKay glared at Fontane through swelling eyes already turning a deep purple. He spat more blood through his cut lip. "What did he do to you, Fontane? Were you so sick and twisted when you got here?"

Fontane pulled back, slightly stunned by the question. "I was a *child*," he said. "My *father* left me here with Marvin Carlton and the other boys. Even his own son had been beaten and starved and savagely abused."

"Adam…"

Fontane nodded solemnly. "Yes. He had been turned out into the general population a few years before I arrived, and by the time I was abandoned here, he was my only saving grace."

"Adam saved you?"

"Adam *taught* me," Fontane said. "He showed me how to survive, gave me the skills I needed to live in this hell hole."

"He taught you to hurt the others."

"To hurt before I could *be* hurt," Fontane said, spitting the words into McKay's face with pure venom.

His eyes glazed over as painful memories flooded his mind. "The things they did to me at first—the boys waiting for me in the shower, in the darkness at lights out, in this barn… My first day, I was beaten so badly, they took me to the infirmary, and the things they had done to me… I begged the nurse to let me die.

"After a year of that, I was a shell, nothing inside me left to call human. And then Adam came to me. He made me whole again, taught me what I needed to be stronger and smarter than the others."

"Is that how he turned the others?"

"You mean Adam's little plan? I had nothing to do with that. Those boys arrived at the end of my time in camp. Adam could see the writing on the wall. His little experiment was his way of getting revenge, finding boys like me—like I was—and using pain and pleasure to make them his own pets. They were weak and vulnerable."

"They were your friends."

"I have no friends," Fontane said with disdain.

"That made it easier to turn from tortured to torturer…" There was a strange ring of pity in McKay's voice.

Again, Fontane was in his battered face. "I became a survivor."

"You became a monster."

In a flash, the sharp-edged knife was at McKay's throat, shaking with the rage behind it. McKay's eyes remained steady on Fontane's face.

Then he heard it…a footstep just outside the walls. *Who?*

Fontane looked back at McKay, who remained oblivious. *Of course, she'd come, crazy woman.* He had no idea how she figured it out before he had time to clean up his tracks, but it didn't surprise him.

"Well, well, Marcus, it seems your little pixie has come to rescue you." Fontane turned away from McKay and slipped warily toward the far corner, where the wall had decayed to the point that he could slip through.

"No! Trilby, he knows you're here! Run!"

Should have gagged him, fool. Fontane fired from the hip as he disappeared into the dark to find his newest problem. The bullet slammed into McKay's chest, and he blacked out.

Trilby had reached the barn walls just as McKay cried out. She saw Fontane turn to shoot McKay and bit her lip to keep from crying out. As he slipped through the barn wall into the darkness, she slipped inside. Surprisingly stealthy in her vest and gun belt, she holstered her Sig Sauer and grabbed her knife. Soon, she was half-catching McKay and lowering him to the dirt floor.

As her ears focused on every sound outside the barn walls, she sent a silent prayer heavenward. McKay was unconscious and bleeding heavily. She removed her uniform shirt and packed it over his wound then used the rope that had held him aloft to tie it in place.

"Don't you die on me, McKay," she whispered fiercely, kissing his forehead as she replaced her knife and grabbed the cell phone from her belt.

"Gwen?" she said, barely above a whisper as she pulled her Sig.

She was relieved to hear the reply. "I've got you, Trilby. EMS en route. Carlsen 15 minutes out."

Without answering, Trilby clipped the phone on her belt and slipped back through the barn wall. She squatted outside allowing her eyes to adjust to the darkness and listening for the sound of

Fontane in the dry brush that overran the property. Her patrol unit blocked escape in McKay's car, but she started in that direction anyway before a cold, hard voice stopped her in her tracks. "You are so much more trouble than you're worth."

"So I've heard," Trilby said, honing in on his voice and shifting direction slightly.

"I knew I should have taken care of you; not left you to Adam."

Trilby shifted again. The voice was closer. She tried to relax the grip on her gun as adrenaline coursed through her. *Breathe, Trilby. Listen. Get Fontane out of the way so EMS can come in, then get back to Marcus.*

"If it weren't for the two of you meddling where you didn't belong…" Fontane's voice held a razor-sharp edge to it. "You don't know what happened here. You don't know—"

"So, tell me, Fontane," Trilby said, as she edged around her patrol unit; he was close. "Tell me what made boys into monsters."

"He did!" Fontane fired from his position behind the trunk of a large oak tree only yards away. She heard the bullet hit her patrol car and imagined it lodging somewhere in her engine. Before he could step back, she fired, hitting him in the shoulder.

He screamed in outrage, and Trilby braced herself. *There it is; there's the crazy we saw in all the others.*

"You little— I'll kill you!" Something in David Fontane snapped, and he ran at her full-tilt, firing wildly.

Trilby rolled out from behind her unit, firing at Fontane's erratic movements, and felt a bullet whiz past her ear. She sent another shot into his upper thigh, but he never slowed. As she came to rest, she squeezed off three more shots, center mass, and Fontane fell face-first into the dirt.

Trilby waited a beat, and when Fontane didn't move, she raced back to McKay without a second thought. Behind her, she heard the sirens of the SWAT team, and soon Carlsen was at her back. "Ambulance, Mike."

"Right behind us. Gwen gave us a heads up as soon as she heard shots fired. They were a whole lot closer than we were."

As if summoned, the barred barn doors burst open, and EMS hurried in with a gurney, the frazzled Sheriff's deputy in tow. It was a county rig, and Trilby knew them all well. "Get him on the stretcher and get him in the rig. He took one to the chest, and we'll figure the rest out en route."

She got no argument from the medics; the sheer amount of blood on both McKay and Trilby told them all they needed to know on scene. He was loaded and in transport in five minutes. Trilby left Carlsen to deal with the mess left behind.

CHAPTER NINETEEN

DAY TEN

The doors swung wide, bright light splashing onto the pavement as a mammoth EMT propelled the stretcher inside. Kelly, the paramedic, worked the bag over McKay's pale white face as Trilby straddled him to continue compressions. Bull pushed them both into the ER.

"Gunshot wound to the chest, lost pulse in the ambulance as we pulled in!" Bull yelled to the attending, who grabbed the foot of the stretcher and directed them to Bed 5.

When they pulled up next to the gurney, Trilby hopped off and assisted with the lift and transfer before being pushed aside by nurses ready to take over. She moved just far enough back to the foot of the gurney to watch as they worked to get him back. She wound up in the ER with a number of her calls, so she was known and respected by the staff. No one tried to move her.

So much blood. Her emergency medical training had kicked in as she rode along in the ambulance, and since Kelly was bigger than Trilby, it had seemed natural for her to top the stretcher to continue compressions. Adrenaline and experience had kept her mind occupied and off the fact that the blood on her hands and uniform was his.

"Hold compressions!" They had given him Epi and now

administered the first shock. Everyone stood clear in anticipation as the doctor applied the paddles.

"I've got a pulse." *The nurse—Trilby knew her name, what was it? Janice.*

Trilby looked to the monitor—the first time her eyes had left his body since she climbed in the rig with him. *Sinus rhythm.*

She breathed in, standing with her arms crossed, and released her death grip on her biceps. Faintly, she felt the pain there; there would be bruises.

A hand landed on her shoulder, and she turned to see Carlsen's face. He must have taken her car and followed. She looked back at McKay, the bag gone, breathing on his own.

"He's strong, Trilby. He's gonna make it."

She looked to the physician for assurance. *He's so young; how long has he been out of school?* She couldn't catch his eye. They were ready to take McKay to surgery.

Carlsen gently pulled her back into the hallway as the gurney rolled by. She reached out, letting her hand brush over him as he passed. "Don't you die on me, Marcus."

When he was gone, she looked up into Carlsen's face, and he pulled her into a hug. "Let's get some coffee. They'll let us wait in the break room; more private."

She followed numbly. She reached for the coffee with hands that didn't seem like her own, saw the blood and turned to the sink along the wall to wash them, scrubbing at them viciously to remove the gore and return a feeling of wholeness.

Carlsen reached around her to shut off the water, dried her hands and turned her from the sink. He handed her the coffee, and she let him guide her to the sofa. He sat beside her and snapped his fingers in front of her face. She turned to him.

"Come to, Trilby. I get what you're going through, but I need you here. I need to know what happened."

Her expression was blank.

"Trilby!" He shook her. "Focus!"

Hot coffee poured out over her hand, the burning sensation finally reaching her shocked mind.

Her voice held ice. "Where's Fontane?"

"Daniel is on the way out to the scene to collect him."

She nodded; no remorse.

"And McKay's car?"

Carlsen could stifle a chuckle. "Still at the scene while evidence is collected, but it's well-guarded, and I warned the rookie in charge of babysitting that his job—and his life—depended on the chief getting it back unharmed."

Trilby nodded. "Good. Ok. Who's running the show?"

"Um… I guess you are."

She looked at him blankly for half a second, blinked and seemed to come to. "Ok. If you haven't already, send a CSU to the Grant Hotel. Fontane must have been meeting Adam Carlton. I want every lead that room has to give us."

"I called for a team on my way to Parker. We should get a report soon."

☐

Trilby set up operations in the staff breakroom. She wouldn't leave the hospital while Marcus was in surgery, and she trusted her guys to get the job done once they had orders to follow. Adam Carlton's hotel room had surrendered no leads; the man was a master at covering his tracks. CSU had also processed Fontane's room with similar results. Her guys were still working the scene in Parker, but it was dark even with the lights they brought in. The FBI were sending a team in the morning to go over everything again and see what other resources they could offer to clean up a mess that had their name all over it.

Trilby was on the radio taking a report when Gwen walked into the room. "What are you doing here, Gwen? You look like you're in pain."

Gwen waved her away. "Where did you expect me to be?" She sat beside Trilby and lifted her coffee-scorched hand.

"Get me a nurse."

"I'm fine." Trilby yanked her hand free and turned back to her laptop and radio.

"I didn't ask you a question; I gave you an order. If you don't want me taking you off the active duty list, you will follow it." Gwen's voice was concerned, but stern.

Trilby stared at her for a moment, then walked to the door and stuck her head out to ask a nurse to step in.

Gwen smiled at the woman in pale blue scrubs. "Hello, Macy, could you get me some peroxide and gauze, please, burn gel, and tape, too."

Macy looked at Trilby's hand, shook her head at the officer and disappeared. It didn't take her long to return with the required items and assist in bandaging the second-degree burn.

Once finished, Gwen leaned back on the couch and looked at her weary friend. "Talk to me, pal."

"I'm busy, Gwen."

Instead of threatening her again, Gwen laid a hand softly on top of Trilby's good one. "How is he?"

Tears rimmed Trilby's eyes when she turned to look at the doctor. "I don't know. He took one to the chest. They took him into surgery to repair damage to his lung. He came in pulseless; lost a lot of blood. Left the ER in sinus and breathing."

Gwen simply waited.

"It was horrible, Gwen. That monster hung him up and beat him. Cut him. And then shot him."

"How long has he been in surgery?"

"Two hours. I'm going crazy, Gwen."

Gwen leaped to her feet and headed toward the door. "Well, let's just see what I can find out." She winked back at her friend. "Breathe, Trilby. I've got your back."

Trilby was at her wit's end, and it had been twenty minutes since Gwen disappeared to find out about McKay.

"Fifty-nine reporting."

She lifted the hand-held radio off the table to respond. "Go ahead, Mike."

"We've done all we can out here until daylight, and these guys are gonna need a break before then so they can get back to it."

Trilby rubbed her forehead. He was right. It was nearly 4 a.m.; dawn was not far off.

"Mike, call it. Round everybody back up there at first light, and make sure you've got dogs and crime scene techs."

"Will do. Any word from CSU at the Grant?"

"Didn't find much in Holmes's room to prove he's Carlton, nothing to give us any idea about what he's up to next. There's nothing in the system on him—he's a ghost.

"And Michael—the bellboy—hasn't been seen since the end of his shift last night. I've got units searching the area for Carlton and the kid, but I'm not holding my breath on finding either…at least not finding the boy alive."

The thought sickened her, and she could hear the sadness in Carlsen's voice as well. Making use of the secure channel, she knew he had to ask, "Hey, Trilby, the guys are all going crazy with worry…"

Of course, they were. McKay wasn't just her chief. "He's still in surgery… Gwen went to get more information, but…"

The beautiful doctor stepped in at that moment, a surgeon in tow.

"Surgeon's here." Trilby dropped the radio on the sofa and looked up at the doctor with her hands gripped in silent prayer.

"You can tell them their chief is going to pull through. He's one tough customer. Bullet missed his heart, nicked a lung, and we repaired it. He's going to be out of commission for a while, but he'll be fine."

Breathe, Trilby.

"Yess!" She hadn't realized the radio landed so it was still keyed. Mike must have heard every word, and not five minutes later, she heard the whoops and hollers of her fellow officers.

"Thank you, Doctor." Tears streamed down her face unbidden.

As the surgeon left, Gwen moved to sit beside Trilby, catching her as she collapsed into the embrace.

"Breathe, Trilby," Gwen whispered as she rocked her friend. "Let it out; let it go."

After some moments, Trilby pulled back and wiped her face.

148

"How soon can I see him?"

"He's in recovery, but the surgeon said about an hour."

"Will he be awake?"

Gwen raised an eyebrow. "He'll be coming out of anesthesia."

"Good. I've got a few choice words for that idiot."

Gwen laughed. "Perhaps you should give him a little recovery time before you lash out." She stood and pulled Trilby to her feet. "I suggest you go home and take a shower. It might be best if he didn't open his eyes to see you covered in his blood."

Trilby looked down at the crusted blood across the front of her uniform. "Oh, that's gonna leave a stain."

"And you smell. Really."

Trilby laughed. "Thanks, Doc, but I'm not leaving Marcus."

"You are, actually. Doctor's orders. He's about to be up to his eyebrows in armed officers coming to make sure what they heard on the radio is the real deal. He's safe as a kitten."

She began to walk Trilby toward the door. "You, on the other hand, will take a unit with you."

"I hardly think I need a babysitter, Gwen."

Gwen turned Trilby sharply to face her. "It was one thing when the crazy Dr. White said Adam Carlton was coming for you, but that has now been confirmed by the diabolical FBI agent. This is not a debate. You will take a unit, and they will come inside with you and stay with you."

Trilby stared hard into Gwen's eyes for a moment, bent on being stubborn, but the genuine concern there won out.

"I'll take Mike. He owes me," she said, looking down at her hand. "And he can come as far as the kitchen to wait while I shower."

"Deal." Gwen hugged her so tight she could hardly breathe. She opened the door to usher Trilby out just as Carlsen reached for the knob to walk in.

"Sergeant Carlsen, wonderful. I have a task for you."

CHAPTER TWENTY

DAY TEN, MID-MORNING

Trilby reluctantly let Carlsen chauffeur her home to shower and change. As they turned out of the hospital parking lot, she sighed and relaxed against the seat. Silently, she thanked God for the miracles of the day.

Carlsen looked at her out of the corner of his eye. "Tough one today, huh?"

"We almost lost him, Mike. I should have seen it, I should have known…"

"How the heck were you supposed to know some FBI guy you never met or spoke to from an entirely different area would be connected to your seemingly unconnected rash of murders? You think you're psychic?"

She cringed. "I thought I was crazy."

"Look, Gwen told me about the dreams, and I don't get it any more than you do. It would spook the daylights out of me. But maybe it's like Gwen said—some part of that big brain of yours figured things out faster than the rest of you.

"Either way, you figured it out in time to save McKay and take down the bad guy."

"*A* bad guy." Trilby shook her head. "He was just one of the boys. Maybe he was worse—maybe a bigger part of the evil out at that wretched place—but he didn't create that travesty of justice, and he didn't put this plan in motion."

"You mean the old man at the hotel? How much trouble can he make now that we know his secrets?"

She gave him a hard look. "That old man is a monster like we've never seen, Mike." She grabbed his arm, desperate to get her point across.

"Do not underestimate him." She accentuated every word, then leaned back into the seat. "We have no idea how many boys there were or how he triggers whatever it is he put in them, but I guarantee you, if we don't put an end to Adam Carlton, the killing will go on."

☐

He watched her climb into the patrol car with what he assumed was her bodyguard. *Smart not to take me for granted, Trilby.* From the moment she stuck her nose into his affairs, he had intended to pay her a special visit—once the plan was finished. Then she killed David. No one took what was Adam Carlton's. He had come to make that clear, and now it was a lesson she would learn as well.

He pulled boy's car into traffic some lengths behind the patrol car. "Where are we going, Trilby dearest? Home, perhaps? How delightful. You do have such a lovely little house."

Of course, he had already been there, already made himself at home searching through her things, seeking all her secrets. She'd never be able to tell. No one would. He could see her enjoying a quiet evening on the porch swing, under that quaint blanket. He sat there, himself, anticipating a time when he could pose her lifeless corpse on that swing and leave her for her *chief* to find.

☐

He had posed the boy, too. *So sweet, so naïve; he never saw it coming.* Carl had showered Michael Kahn with attention and gifts each time Michael attended to him at the Grant Hotel. He had delighted in the sparkle that came into the boy's eyes with each new present. *It was so easy to earn his affection, so easy to earn his trust.*

He made sure Michael would think nothing of playing chauffeur to the elderly Mr. Holmes in his off-duty hours. The trips slowly grew longer and more remote as Carl entertained the boy with stories of his travels.

And then Michael drove him to a quiet spot by the lake for a sunset picnic. They dined on fine wine and exotic foods, and the boy grew drowsier with each sip. As he began to slip away into unconsciousness, Carl set about tying his hands and feet.

"Worry not, sweet Michael," Carl said with a strange smile. "I'm taking you home."

☐

Adam Carlton never underestimated an opponent—until now—and it made his blood boil. All his planning ruined by one, tiny woman. He watched as the patrol car pulled into her driveway and the two went inside. Then he drove further down the street and parked the car. He walked into the woods behind the neighborhood and backtracked to Trilby's house, and the window he left open in the guest bedroom.

Surprisingly nimble for an old man—that's what they would say. He hoisted himself inside without a sound and listened for movement in the house. Knowing the door was silent, he cracked it open to look across and down the hall toward the kitchen, where the uniformed cop sat at the bar waiting. Adam heard Trilby start the shower and smiled with pure venom.

He eased into the hallway. The officer was focused on guarding Trilby against intruders on the outside, his back turned slightly to the hallway. He turned just in time for Adam to hit him with Trilby's old tactical baton—part of the bounty gathered in his earlier treasure hunt in Trilby's house. He caught the officer as he slumped and quietly lowered him to the ground.

"Mike?"

Adam turned like a trapped animal ready to pounce. She was calling from the bedroom.

"There's some sodas in the fridge if you want one. I won't be long."

With the utmost care, Adam removed the officer's handcuffs and cuffed him to the foot railing of the kitchen bar. He grabbed the tactical baton, sliding it into the pocket of his coat as he took out a long, slim knife—one of his favorites.

"Ah, Trilby," he whispered, as he stalked down the hall. "Let's play…"

As he reached for the doorknob, a cell phone began to ring in the kitchen.

"Hey, Mike! That's mine, will you grab it?"

Adam slipped the knife back into his pocket and braced himself against the wall, waiting for the inevitable.

☐

Trilby heard her phone ringing and wondered if Carlsen had heard her. She had just finished dressing in a T-shirt and jeans and opened the door to yell down the hall. "Mike? I'm drying my hair. Can you get—"

Carlton grabbed her and slammed her against the wall, holding her there with both hands around her throat. Her feet flailed several inches off the ground. "I'm afraid *Mike* is indisposed."

Trilby's eyes went wide as she clawed at the hands around her throat. She reached up, trying to get to Carlton's eyes, but he pulled his head away. She tried bringing her arms down against his to break his hold, but he was deceptively strong.

As she neared unconsciousness, he released her throat and grabbed her by the hair with one hand. In the other, she suddenly saw something shiny.

As he dragged her past Carlsen's body in the kitchen, she gasped for the air she had been deprived of and kicked at Carlsen, hoping to see some sign of life. "Mike!" she tried to scream, but it came out a pathetic squeak. There was a pool of blood around his head.

She heard the patio door open, and then Carlton flung her to the concrete floor like a ragdoll. He stood over her menacingly, and she saw the shiny object was a slim, deadly knife. He caressed it with a sickening fondness.

"Trilby Baines, at last. You have been quite a thorn in my side, young lady."

Trilby tried to sit up, but he kicked her in the chest, propelling her onto her back again. "What did you do to Mike?"

"That is hardly of any consequence right now. Pay attention." He was agitated, fidgety. "Time is not on my side, *Trilby.* You've ruined everything, and now I haven't even got the time to teach you a proper lesson."

"A lesson?"

He kneeled on her chest, crushing the breath from her again and putting his face within inches of hers. "No one takes what belongs to Adam Carlton."

"I…was right. That's…what this…was about…" she gasped, "those men…getting even?"

He straddled her torso so she could take a breath, pinning her arms beside her. "Of course."

"And me, I need to be punished for getting in the way?"

"No, you needed to be removed for getting in the way." He slid the knife to her throat. "You need to be punished for taking what was mine."

She stared back at him with no fear, prayer running through her mind. "David."

"Yes, David." The knife pressed into her flesh as he spat the words in her face.

"He must have been your favorite creation."

Carlton laughed. "I didn't create David, I loved him, helped him to become himself."

"And the others?"

"Bait."

Trilby's mind raced. "Bait? …For David. You wanted him back here—back to Parker and back to you."

Carlsen's phone began to ring. "They're looking for us."

"Yes. As I said, no time." He pressed the knife against her throat again. "A pity, really. You deserve more…for David."

Trilby's prayers whispered past her lips, but as her situation grew darker, her thoughts became harder to control. Prayers became scripture—promises she held to be true.

"The Lord is my shepherd…"

"What? What foolishness is that, Trilby? Are you calling on

your *God* now? I've been to hell and back, and I can tell you there is no God."

Adam and Trilby were locked in their own world, the only sound her whispered prayers. Neither heard the front door open. His eyes never left Trilby's face until they heard the gunshot. He turned toward the sound, and the bullet hit his chest, throwing him backward and off of Trilby. She scrambled away, then looked up to see Gwen kneeling over Carlsen. Still shaky, she crawled toward the doctor.

Sirens echoed in the distance. "Gwen?"

Gwen applied pressure to Carlsen's head wound with a towel she found on the kitchen counter. With one hand, she tipped Trilby's face up to look at her. "Are you ok?"

"I am *so* glad I taught you how to use a pistol."

Gwen kissed Trilby's forehead. "Oh, sister, so am I."

"How's Mike?"

"That…" She threw a venomous look toward Adam Carlton's lifeless body. "He gave Mike's skull a good blow, lots of blood, but head wounds bleed like crazy, you know that. There's an ambulance on the way, so we'll get him off to the ER, and he should be fine."

Trilby rested her head on Gwen's knee. "How did you know?"

"You left me in charge of Marcus and then didn't answer your phone? Are you kidding me?"

Trilby looked up then. "Marcus? Is something…"

"No, no. He's fine. Charlene from dispatch is sitting with him, swatting away all the others so he can rest."

"Charlene can be mean. I wouldn't tangle with her."

"Me, either," Gwen said, helping Trilby to her feet as the EMTs rushed in to work on Mike. "We also got word from CSU when they got back out to Parker. Once the sun came up, they did a sweep of the whole camp… They found Michael Kahn's body in one of the bedrooms of the old Carlton home. From what I heard, it wasn't a pretty picture."

"Kahn—the bellboy, right?" Trilby's stomach lurched.

"Right. Officer Cooper was out there keeping an eye on things. He said the kid was tortured before being killed and posed in Adam Carlton's bedroom."

Trilby sat on the bumper of Carlsen's patrol car so Gwen could get a better look at her.

As she cleaned the cut above Trilby's eye, she said, "By the way, McKay was awake when I left. And asking for you."

"Gwen!" Trilby dashed toward Gwen's car, waiting impatiently for the good doctor to catch up. Once inside, she paused in her excitement. "Thank you, Lord, my strength and my shield."

Gwen gave her a smile and started the engine. "Amen."

CHAPTER TWENTY-ONE

DAY TEN, AFTERNOON

When Marcus woke again, Charlene was gone. He knew the tiny hand holding his and reached to touch the soft red hair. Trilby had fallen asleep in the chair beside him, her head lying on his forearm. When he moved, she turned her sleepy eyes in his direction.

He lifted her bruised face. "What… Did Fontane do that? What happened?"

"Carlton actually, but it's a really long story." As she sat up more, he saw her neck ringed in dark purple bruises.

"Trilby!" He tried to sit up, but pain shot through him, and he collapsed on the bed.

She put her hand on his chest. "Marcus, breathe. I'm fine. I promise it looks worse than it is."

"Tell me."

"You'll get a full report, Chief, as soon as you're up to it. For now, just know the case is resolved, and all officers are accounted for. Mike took a thumping, and he's occupying a bed down the hall for a while, but we're all alive, and it's done."

McKay reached to touch her face. "If I lost you…"

"I know the feeling, Marcus," she said, taking his hand and kissing it.

"Trilby…"

"No. No, Marcus. Don't. Don't you push me away for my own good. Not now." Tears flowed down her face as she held his hand to her lips.

"Come here."

She looked up at him then and moved closer. He patted the bed beside him, and she curled against him, her head resting gingerly on the uninjured side of his chest. His steady heartbeat calmed her.

"I've been trying to talk to you for days. I don't want to push you away." He kissed the top of her head, and she turned her face up to look at him.

"What are you saying, Marcus?"

"You know me better than anyone, Trilby. You should know how much I need you. It's true, we aren't who we were then—either of us."

She held her breath but remained quiet.

"The only time I have ever felt whole was when you were with me, and the only time I have ever felt alive was in your arms. I know a gift when I see one, Trilby Baines, and I'm not giving this one back—not ever again." He looked into her eyes for a long moment. "We're going to do it right, this time, Trilby."

She smiled, tears welling up in her eyes again.

He looked away then. "Well, this is certainly no place for a proper proposal, so you'll have to wait on that, but just don't you give up on me."

Trilby rose up enough to kiss him softly. "Not a chance, Chief."

CHAPTER TWENTY-TWO

FOUR MONTHS LATER

She breathed in the scent of honeysuckle and felt his arms slip around her waist, his chest warm against her back.

"Trilby." His breath tickled her ear. "Come inside."

He kissed her neck, but alarm rose in the pit of her stomach. *Not again. Not Marcus.*

Something hit her in the chest, and she felt wetness on her cheek. She raised her hands to defend herself as her eyes flew open.

"Mojo, no!" The too-affectionate white pit bull stood with one paw in the middle of Trilby's chest as he tried to lick his new owner. Trilby had no idea how the dog had gotten into the hammock in the first place. It was a relief to learn the warm breath and "kissing" had been more real than dream, even if her neck was wet with dog slobber.

Laughter sounded from the doorway of the casita. "Mojo, down." The dog instantly obeyed.

"Why does he obey you and not me?" Trilby asked with no small amount of petulance.

"Because he knows you don't mean it." McKay pulled Trilby to her feet and circled his arms around her waist. She turned her face up to his.

He smiled down at her, softly kissing her forehead, then the end of her nose and her cheek before brushing his lips against hers. She rose up on her tiptoes to intensify the kiss, sliding her arms around his neck and pulling him down to her. His arms held her tightly.

When they pulled apart, she laughed breathlessly. "Maybe we should go inside, Mr. McKay, before the neighbors get a real show."

McKay swept her off her feet and carried her through the door of their getaway, closing it behind him with a kick just after Mojo skittered through. "I believe you're right, Mrs. McKay.

He fell with her onto the king-sized bed and held her close, kissing her deeply. When he pulled back, he ran his fingers through her unruly crimson hair. She had only looked more beautiful once— as she had walked down the aisle of that little church on Carlsen's arm.

"I love you, Trilby, even more than I imagined I could." Her smile electrified her bright blue eyes, and he sighed. "I'm sorry it took me so long to get here."

"No worries, Chief. You were worth the wait."

THE END

ABOUT THE AUTHOR

Jennings has been a writer of words in one form or another for her entire career—whether as a print journalist, a marketing specialist or a trainer designing custom programs.

For several years, she set aside her personal writing career to assist other authors in achieving their dreams through her work with Lone Mesa Publishing. **PROGRAMMED** is her first published work and the first in the **Trilby Baines Thrillers**. It draws on her years working with law enforcement and emergency services as a reporter and a decade serving as a firefighter/EMT.

In addition to her love of police procedurals and all things suspense, Jennings has rediscovered her love of the outdoors. She chronicles her hiking exploits on the Instagram (txhikergirl) and in her blog at http://fortyfithiker.online.

www.ingramcontent.com/pod-product-compliance
Lightning Source LLC
Chambersburg PA
CBHW070927130626
46555CB00001B/321